This book is a work of fiction situations are the product of the author's imagination. Any resemblance to actual persons living or dead, or historical events, locales, or organizations is purely coincidental.

Mr. Tell Me Anything

ISBN 13
9781505892758

ISBN 10
1505892759

Printed in USA

For information address CPTM Media, Publishing Company.

CPTM Media
www.cptmmedia.com

Dedication

This book is for my mother, Maxine Yvette Robinson. You fought a good fight. I will meet you in the clouds someday. In the meantime, rock Sierra Simone for me. And thank you for a fine introduction to my Lord and personal Savior. I love you more with each day that passes and I honor you with this piece.

TABLE OF CONTENTS

Acknowledgements

I would like to thank my very wise father, Julius Alfred Robinson Sr., who carried a very large portion of my heart with him into heaven. I honor you for the blue print you set before me. You always encouraged me to become a greater woman than ever imagined. I wish you could have stayed a little while longer. You are gone but never forgotten.

I thank God above all others; He has truly made all the difference. I am so glad I met you, Jesus. And I am thankful for my hardships that sent me racing to your open arms. Hallelujah!

I must also acknowledge my very loving and brand new husband, Reginald A. Robinson Sr. You have been a rock! You came and scooped me up! Love you, baby.

I cannot forget my sons, Lorenzen, Jr. and the twins Lamar and Shamar plus little Lawson who we call "Big Law." These are men like no others! Blessed and a blessing.

Words cannot express my admiration and love for my eldest daughter, Loren, whose face drove me to desire "good things" for my future. You are a jewel! You never cease to inspire me with your joyful spirit, Mama.

I love you, Miss Sofia, my "happy ending" to motherhood. Keep on dreaming and praising God. That sure is a pretty name.

Acknowledgements (Cont.)

A world of gratitude to my Pastor, O.E. Finley for believing in me when it seemed as though the whole world was against me....Love you!

Thank you, Mrs. Jones, my first grade teacher at Westwood Elementary. You let me write all your lessons on that chalkboard and inspired my hands.

My deepest gratitude goes to all my siblings who always stood closely by, even if it was just to catch me.

Thank you, Janice Taylor and France Robinson. She can never be replaced but you've done more than your part in trying. Love you guys. God Bless You.

Finally, Nicolle and the crew over at CPMT Media, I could not have done this without you. You have been irreplaceable!

.

"Tell them "next" because you can't find your soul mate
if you're spending too much of your life on someone
else."
Sherra Wright

"People are who they are!"
A.D. Taylor

"People say that love endures all things, but does the
body hold the same truth? Let your love be good to your
body."
Sherra Wright-Robinson

Introduction

We all know at least "one" like him.....A Mr. Tell Me Anything. All you have to do is look at your past, be honest about your future or examine your present......he's right there. He's that "one" who no doubt always offered or offers you "words." And it's often explicitly all the words that you yearn to hear. He does it at a level of simplicity, too. After all, he's clever enough to not be discovered. He perpetrates until he's positioned himself and often implanted his seeds into your body and your family tree. Ultimately successful, your way of thinking is often seduced, causing your every instinct to become a second-guessing game. He has you.....you are rattled. You are under his command, girl.

So you say to yourself...."What's wrong with me?" Why can't I shake this man? There is nothing wrong. You've fell in love. And that's exactly what this very planet has taught us to do.....FALL. We fall for that other human being that causes our hair to stand up on the back of our necks. It's kind of natural.

Don't fall too hard though. This is what Sharon Roberson teaches us through her trials and pain. She's the main character. You would think this story was about a man but it's not about him.....It's about a woman that needed help.

My hope is that this story, though fictional, will help someone else who does not have the strength to carry on or who feels "defeated "for wanting to do so.

I believe there is a woman somewhere out there that is waiting to hear this story because she's tired. There is another one out there just looking for the gossip because she's bored. But there are many who need Sharon and her experiences to encourage themselves to break the chains holding them down because they are totally miserable.

Someone needs to know that God loves them and that He is always waiting for you to take the first step.....no matter what. He wants to hear from you.

Sharon found herself crying out for help on more than one occasion, like me. And she wasn't even close to perfect, like me. But she knew something had to change. Why? Because she gathered that there was something absolutely missing, like me.

Don't keep crying........Jesus didn't die for that! Trust me.....Sharon found it out the hard way.

Prologue

Before he finds himself in the presence of Sharon Roberson, Mr. Tell Me Anything enjoys the stardom of being known as a prominent basketball player in his hometown of Mississippi. But his travels and his perfectly chiseled face would eventually afford him the opportunity to meet her.

It was love and hate at the very first sight. He hated that she was all he had been warned she would be. She hated that her interest was officially sparked by a minor. They both loved that they had found a friend in one another.

Sharon needs to decide what she will do next to regain her life after her Mama's death. He needs to decide how he will measure up and capture her as his own with an age difference and struggling budget. His laughter and love causes her to pause for a moment and see what she has been missing.

CHAPTER 1
THE TAKEOVER

It was such a gorgeous day outside, almost as if God, in all His majesty, was directly smiling down on Sharon Roberson. She could really use some happiness these days, with life's new presentation of sorrow and absolute grief. So, while the blazing rays of the sunshine were taking a much needed day off in the wonderful month of May, she found herself taking advantage of the brief moment of silence on her rear terrace.

The clear blue skies were filled with fresh warm air that made her laden heart feel slightly lighter for the first time in several months. She could feel the crisp breeze whisk through her wide opened nostrils as she stretched her narrow neck a little further towards the brilliant heavens. Before she drifted completely off into the most serene place available in her deeply troubled mind, she caught a quick glimpse of the clock above the kitchen stove peeking through the patio doors. It read half past 11:00 am. She could remember him tell her that he'd be there around 10:30. So *what was the holdup*? He was actually never late for anything in her life. Mr. Roberson, her father, was quite the contrary, ordinarily a stickler on punctuality and making his appointments. She was always the one keeping his organized nerves on sharpened edge with her consistent tardiness. In a word.........Little Miss Roberson was practically late for everything in her life thus far.

"I guess he chooses to be late today on my first time being *on* time for anything ......priceless. "Nothing in her bleak life was going right anyways. So, she waited. "I will wait. But I hate waiting. It feels like I'm wasting away here. I want to go home. "

Sharon had made an honest attempt this particular morning though to be on time, while soaking up the element so vividly displayed by the smooth movement of air and the sun's inspiration.

In all her admiration, she tried not to focus on thinking back to the reason she had even called her father in the first place. Just last week, she had spoken to him in the middle of the night. On her bed of sorrow, she explained how her grades had plummeted so low that she managed to receive her very own first academic probation letter. The university had happily volunteered to add to the severity of her growing depression with their carefully drafted overly informative document. She had precisely related to him what it contained and that she really needed to move home because of it. With something so unambiguously positioned in her student file, she seemed to have been forced into a corner. The paperwork bombshell concluded that her once *hefty scholarship* would be "revoked" if she didn't pull up her grades immediately and it also stated that she had already succeeded in forfeiting a huge portion of the funds allotted because of recent scores that were submitted to them. There was a peculiar thing about *this* fiasco.......for once she had no intentions of trying to fix the situation at hand. Her declining energy level was way too dispirited for that. Sharon had chosen all on her own to quit! This was normally not one of her preferred things to do, but in this case, a very necessary option to pursue for the distraught student. She was exhausted.

She had successfully proven herself to be a previous "fixer" all of her life on numerous occasions, always offering self-proclaimed solutions to everyone else's issues. Often, she practiced this function despite the self-sacrifice to be rendered, ending up with virtually no compensation at all. But this time......*No*.

"It takes way too much vivacity to tackle things over and over again. I am not gonna spend my precious time trying to piece *my* boggled mind back together....doesn't seem to work on *me* anyway. Besides, it doesn't matter.....it won't bring her back! "

She had to admit to herself that it was much easier to help outsiders at this point. Their problems were not like *her* problems. Before her Mama got sick, she had had none of any real magnitude. But now, in the blink of an eye and nine weeks of agony, she was totally shattered. She had to depart from this place where she now functioned like a zombie. Sharon really needed to go home.

"Yes, Home Sweet Home. "Memphis, Tennessee was all she could think of these days. Her family would all be there ready with open arms. There were her cousins and those who had also missed her Mama, too. Maybe she could share her pain with a familiar spirit, someone who loved her like she did....till their stomach hurt deep down on the inside..... This was another disease that the doctors couldn't cure. Or there was the slight possibility that visiting her grave would give her some sense of closure. She would try anything at this point. The pain was way too great!

"What's taking him so long?"

The agonizing death of her mother took its toll on everybody in their family as it progressed to striking her down, too. Things were so different without her to call or speak anything into her life. She was an expert at teaching Sharon and her siblings as children to know *how* they should move ahead in life and what avenues to take in doing so. Her knowledge was second to none, always being Spirit led. Sharon wished she could be more like her; she longed for a piece of her sound insight at this moment in her life. Remembering her Mama, she paced back and forth wanting so desperately to rush into her Dad's strong arms, only to feel him cradle her and hear "I Love You". It wasn't the same as having Mama around but he was always just as encouraging and full of hope as a very strong second option. She hadn't seen him in months now; time had somehow slipped away from them both. Living in Nashville, Tennessee had seemed "right down the street" from Memphis, Tennessee before Mama died. But now the miles stretched out like the Mississippi River, so far and long. And her mind was getting muddier by the minute just thinking of the actual distance present between the two of them. She anticipated just how fast she would race to him and how intense their embrace would be.

"I miss him so much. I wonder what he's going to say and what he's going to be wearing. I bet he's gonna be wearing that ridiculous blue baseball cap." He always thought it made him look younger. It wasn't that he needed that option because he was an old man to be reckoned with. His looks were impeccable. Her Daddy had stood at 6'1" and possessed the most handsome smile a woman could ever encounter. But he had one itsy bitsy deficiency at times......he loved that jaded little cap.

And now he was pulling right up outside her place to rescue her. "Daddy, what took you so long? I have been standing out here for like three years."

In the midst of his laughter and smiles of adoration, she noticed that there was no cap this time and that her Father's head was a lot grayer than she ever recollected. But who could talk? Several patches of hair were absent from her scalp as well. She was thinning. They had both been through the ringer.

"Wow, I thought all this time that I was the only one suffering. Surely, the dull hair color is a clear indication that he has endured many restless nights as well." But of course, the possibility of guilt still lingered as a strong source of his prolonged stress. He had to no doubt be vexed with the fact that he had certain limitations as a husband to her Mama at times. Her father had been very popular with the womenfolk.....all of them, to say the least. But how could she lose focus at a time as crucial as this?

"God tells us to forgive people, right? Besides, Mama is in a better place....right? I could never make it through so many things like she did. She was so strong and brave........a real fighter."

And Lord did she fight? Her Dad had been vicious in his previous endeavors. She could remember this one particular night or morning as clear as day. It was around 4:30 a.m. and her Mama snatched on the bedroom lights as she frantically paced the chilly hallway. She raced back and forth to the living room window, just waiting. Then she could see the dim headlights. It was her Auntie, providing the getaway car. Mama made all three of them, her children, get up. Frightened out of their little twelve and under minds, they were all shoved into the backseat of Auntie's car. Off they went into the night. The sun was still asleep along with every neighbor and what seemed to be every neighborhood.

In all the chaos, her baby brother asks, "Where are we going, Mama?" Mama shrugged him off but Sharon could hear her grumbles underneath her breathe, muffled with sobs, what seemed like a familiar phrase in their household that day and time........ "To catch a liar."

"A what?"

"Your Daddy....just sit back and be quiet till I tell you to talk. Better yet.... go back to sleep."

That was their key to shut up their mouths and enjoy the mission. Mama was normally patient but she meant business this night and they could see it all over her face. Most times when she raised her eyebrow....nobody even breathed. This night they had all wished themselves dead for just a moment until the air was cleared....Mama was hot!

So, there they were racing the streets, scared to death, breathless, when they reach a long hill and were told to "get down" onto the floor of the car. Auntie then shuts out the headlights and Mama jumps right out, walks about fifty feet and hops into her very own light blue Cadillac '78 Fleetwood with white wall tires and whistles ...."Yall, come on. "Right then and there they all race for the back seat and door. Mama and her three small children zoom off into the rising sun and back to their own house. It felt like they were in a Dukes of Hazard Movie or something. But it didn't end there.

"Mama, why are you stealing your own car?"

"Because, it's mine. "He totally should have seen that coming. Everything was hers....your comb, your brush, your room, your clothes.....all hers, according to her.

More even ridiculous though...... her Daddy had parked Mama's brand new Cadillac right smack dead in the middle of his new girlfriend's driveway. Yeah, she was the one who was not supposed to be the girlfriend anymore. But they all knew the ending to that story, same as the one before. Maybe he thought the Cadi to be invisible. Sharon really didn't know, but she knew this.... Her Daddy called bright and early the same morning with his best lie ever told.

"Baby, you won't believe what happened at the plant last night. I came out to the lot after break for a smoke and someone had taken the car. I called the police...I will let you know when I hear something."

"That's strange because I remember going to your slut's house and picking up MY CAR this morning when you had it all up in her driveway. But it's where it belongs now. So, come on. Come get your belongings. I got it all packed and on the front porch!"

The room grew silent as the children listened through the master bedroom door. They could hear her slam the innocent receiver of the phone back into place. Surely it was damaged beyond repair. Seconds later the tears came tumbling down. He had done it again and she had let him.

Though the years had passed, Sharon could remember her Mama's pain just like it was yesterday. He was always much better at fathering them as his children. His husband skills needed quite some work. But all she could be concerned about right now was her swift departure under his immediate care and supervision. And he was in route already, yearning to support her measures of escaping. Besides, his indecencies never prevented him from being her perfect Daddy, and a great one at that. But he did make it extremely hard for a brother to approach her at this point, never trusting a man again to a fault. Relationships concerning love were an issue. Because of what she encountered, Sharon found detachment easy, living with a certain degree of paranoia. Meaningless sex was a better fit for her. Though she wanted something more serious eventually, she didn't know how she would start on that path.

"They better come correct....that's all I know."

Her father arrived in the team van, with a U-Haul hooked in behind it. "Yes! " His summer amateur basketball team had a tournament in the city tonight; they would no doubt help him out. Hard work was his middle name and lazy young men were not part of his vocabulary. His plight was to always try to be a mentor of some sort, giving back to the community in any way possible. But in return, his candidates usually had to be loyal and honest.....willing to work for what they wanted out of life. It didn't surprise her that he would have them commit to helping him out.

As her heart ceased fluttering, she detected seven trees standing in her father's shadow, the team. Every one of them was a babe around age seventeen. Oddly, only one of the lads was less than six feet tall. He had brought giants to assist him.

"This outta be really fast." she thought. They resembled timbering oak trees with planks for human feet. "How awkward is that? Where do they buy these children's shoes from? "

"Well, Hello Guys….. I need you to grab all this stuff first. And you….you can grab that over there."

She was standing in the doorway pointing to carefully stacked containers that held mostly keepsakes and precious items, mixed with an assortment of packed boxes. "Be careful with…….."

Once acknowledged, they sprinted past her like they were in some sort of expedition to see who was gonna crash the place first. She recalculated then that this was gonna be a longer day than expected. For a brief moment though she envied their tenacity. They were all full of youth and untainted by the stench of death in their families. They were full of life, preparing to play against a new team in an unknown environment. They were somehow coined brave in her sight for doing so. She wished so desperately that she could feel alive and brave again, too. All her security had been compromised. Relocation *had* to be the key. She thought of meeting new people. She thought of her stepmother–to-be.

"I wonder what she's really like. Does she know who she's marrying? Has he miraculously changed now? Will she love me?" There were so many questions and no answers readily available. The only thing she knew for sure was that her lease was broken and she was surrounded by individuals with large amounts of vibrant life surging right through them.

"I wish all of y'all would quit playing and hurry up so we can finish. We have a game today. "Two of his teammates were throwing around one of her cherished stuffed dolls from childhood. She was her Raggedy Ann with lots of miles on her. But Sharon called her "Dolly." She didn't *play* with her anymore, but her Mama was always committed to keeping her intact by mending her over the span of several years. She was still very well put together. Her Mama was excellent at patching up things. Besides the slight discoloration and a little matted hair on the back of her yarn head, she was as good as new. Sharon always believed that her Mama thought of herself *as* the doll that needed to be worked on. She had a disturbing fascination with the care it took to preserve the little keepsake.....always needing something to rescue from disaster.

And now the teammates were tugging her precious Dolly from each other saying that it was the only thing that they were going to move today. The entire group was previously instructed by her Father, the Assistant Coach, to "do whatever needs to be done." But these teenagers began to perform their duty to her and Dolly, all maintaining an attention span of about ten seconds each. The ones that were not in destructive mode.....they ended up being in slow motion, moving at the slowest pace possible to mankind. They were like a bowl full of lazy!

"Y'all, we are gonna be here all day. Let's get through with this. I'm ready to get out of here."

Sharon bounced by in her favorite cut-off Levi's shorts and a midriff hot pink tank top. She often had the habit of walking on her tippy toes; it was the cutest thing about her still left these days. The older generation of women called her walk a stride. The oldest generation of women, like her grandmother, coined it as "galloping "because of her tremendous height that accompanied it. Her grandmother had sworn that she was a real life stallion and that there was no other little girl like her in the world. And Sharon had believed her. She was wise for God's sake. She knew how old people practically *knew everything about everything*, whether she choose to adopt their ideas or not.

Sharon could sense all the heads in the group turn towards her sculpted calf muscles in the atmosphere. All her strenuous running days had paid off. She deemed exercise as a remedy for stress also. It didn't actually work for her current anxiety though, just helped her get a night's sleep here and there throughout the process. Nonetheless, the definition of the muscles was in full effect as she continued towards the crowd. By now, she was front and center with her abs on display, too. It's crazy, but miniature clothing and shots of tequila somehow evoked a sense of freedom in her.

As she reached the front bedroom, she was trying to gather information regarding the commotion in the next room. Then, the same commanding voice spoke again, "Hey!"

"Hay is for horses. What? "Her mind was fixated on the thought that who told him he could talk to her? He was a member of staff and a teenage one at that. She definitely didn't converse with teenagers under *any* circumstances. She barely even acknowledged her own baby brother, who was soon to be nineteen and actually quite adorable, possessing the same last name. So once again, who told *him* he could address her? She had ignored them all, especially him, even though he was the only annoying one trying to get something done today and physically towered over all the others.

She observed them like a hawk, being cautious not to let their faulty little hands destroy anything inherited from her mother. All her belongings were priceless to Sharon. They were all she had left. Not a single one of them could do anything correct on that morning for this reason....she didn't want them touching her Mama's stuff. To make matters worse, they were late, and then they were unsuccessfully attempting to make up for the expended time by flinging her valuable items into the dusty truck. And all the while, they were sopping up the dazzling sunshine and refreshing breeze, just standing around grinning between each trip back and forth to the vehicle.

"Pathetic, Daddy, they are totally going to break something." She had to convince him of the disaster they were about to impose on her personal property.

"No they are not; just move out of the way. I don't want Danielle to get hurt." She had belonged to her mother for as long as she could remember. But now she had inherited the sole responsibility of raising her alone. Danielle was ultimately beautiful with locks and locks of constricted brown curls. She was the most adorable little thing ever known to their family. This girl had become her best friend in the world now. You couldn't ask for a confidant of her background, born to lend an unbiased ear. She would simply allow her to *spill it all* on her, all without a reply. Though her listening skills were supreme, her touch was even more significant. She had a way of beckoning Sharon over to cuddle with her for extended moments of tranquility. Danielle had become great company as she traveled with her, always at her side. If she couldn't go for some reason, Sharon favorably declined and stayed put at home. She wasn't going to let her out of her sight. Just recently her neighbor decided that he would "walk Danielle" for her and she "accidentally" wandered off about fifty five feet. She had a conniption fit, vowing to never speak to him again. Besides, he was the noisiest and horniest neighbor in the complex, with all his flicks playing through the unfiltered walls. Sharon and her roommate thought that surely he must watch regular television shows periodically. Up to that point, there had been no such thing.....just girls moaning twenty four seven through the thin sheetrock. There was no reason to even elaborate on the sweat that reeled down his forehead when Miss Roberson strolled to the unit's mailbox. He just so happened to be making his run simultaneously when she decided to make her way over there. Danielle, coupled with his irresponsibility was the perfect excuse to rid them both of him at last indefinitely. Clingy men as neighbors had always been a key problem of hers.....

"Maybe he can't help himself. Okay, so I'll give him that much. But nonetheless, him hanging around my door resembling a wreath or a permanent ornament of some sort.....well, that's just simply unacceptable."

"Why are you carrying that stupid dog around with you like she's a real baby or something?" Her thoughts were interrupted by his voice that came forward again.

"Did you just call my mother's dog stupid? You've got some nerve! I want you silly boys out of my place this moment! Get out! You smell like wet puppies and old socks anyway. And why is everything so damned funny? What is so damned funny?"

26

"Does your dad know that you curse? You better be glad he's outside."

"Does your dad know you're *alive*? And why don't you just shut up? That's why you idiots are taking so long, spending too much time laughing and trying to hold conversations with grown people. Not to mention, I caught your friend rummaging through my top underwear drawer while the others were raiding the refrigerator and stealing stuff to drink. This was not part of the deal. No one mentioned comedians, perverts or free drinks with open bars to me! ....Daddy!!!!!!. "

Despite the new circus of the entourage, Sharon decided to put a lid on it as she watched her father struggle with the marble top on the coffee table from the front window. She needed to keep her respect for him clear. She sought sincerely to express her deep gratitude for his taking time to redeem her from the disaster still in progress. His generosity had been far too great for any self-centeredness on her part now. So she bit her tongue, exhaled and stomached it. Besides, soon she would be home and safe from all the destructive thoughts swarming around in her head and the recent wild animals she had indirectly invited into her apartment.

"Daddy, can you tell them not to be so rough with my lamps? And that's my good stuff in that box. Excuse me; she's my mom's ......" In all his boldness, the youngster had reached right out to touch her sweet little puppy and

27

then she bit his ass. Oh, how it made her day! She had wanted all morning to cuss them all out. She wished that she could have chomped them all. For a fleeting moment Sharon imagined her as a renowned Rottweiler on the loose without an owner to be found. It would have been a more perfect scene for her and the intruders. They were all disgusting, immature and noticeably obnoxious.

"A little rabies never killed anyone. How in the world are they gonna win a game today?" she thought. "They · can't even move a queen-sized bed, a sofa and twenty-five medium sized boxes, without constant supervision. They are gonna wear my Daddy's nerves down to the ground. They are soooo sorry."

She wasn't the only one who noticed, either. Danielle had grasped the concept, too. "Good girl," she thought to herself. This team sucked! They traveled all this way to lose. "Poor, Daddy. There is no hope for this group." It was just a matter of time before the hostility would build up and the sweet little puppy would attack all their little lazy asses.

"If only she had a leash, I would cut the strings right now," she chuckled to herself.

After feeling the pain of her vicious bite and the embarrassment of his teammate's gagging, he spoke again. "Damn your dog is just as mean as your stuck up ass."

She couldn't believe her ears now. Did a simple sixteen year old just fix his fresh vocal cords to pronounce

28

her as stuck up? He didn't even know anything about her. He wasn't even supposed to be talking to her at this moment.

"I'm way out of your league….. Stay in your lane, little boy with your overgrown looking ass? Oh my God…… I should have called the professional movers. They don't talk; they just work until they get the job done!" She had a little of her Mama's fortune still left. Mama had recently died of breast cancer just months ago, leaving Sharon her home, not so old blue Pontiac, feisty dog and a decent insurance policy behind.

"He must not know about me," she concluded. "I am not the one to be played with and my toy poodle isn't either. You're not going to talk to either of us like that. I am a whole twenty one years old and this is *our* apartment that you are standing in," she thought.

Suddenly, it occurred to her that after today's date she would no longer have an apartment or open terrace to walk out onto. There would be no silent escape for her on the lounging chair positioned towards the heavens. She would be back in Memphis, living with her Daddy, waiting for the renter to miss one full payment on her Mama's old house that she now solely owned. She was a faithful tenant so far, but one wrong move and she'd be back in hers.

"I'll be back in mines! "In the meantime, her only other option was to avoid getting stuck with some lengthy

29

leasing agreement that she would probably need to break. She did have an older cousin that she could stay with but she wants your ass to disappear when her company comes by (like every day). This she would find ultimately impossible because Sharon Roberson was a female with a truckload of ass. Nonetheless, she was loading up the junk in the trunk, her new guard dog, and all her earthly possessions and headed home this weekend. Everything was intact and perfectly packaged, including her broken heart.

"What are you staring at boy?"

"Nothing…….. absolutely nothing. They already told me about you. They said wait till you see Coach's daughter. She's fine, she got good hair, and she's red and tall and blah, blah, blah…….."

"And?"

"And all kinds of stuff about you, but you ain't that damn pretty because your ass is stuck up and that's a perm!"

"Don't worry about what I am or where I get my touchups, you just be the good little slave that you are and put those damn boxes in that truck like my Daddy told you to!"

And he did, all the while hysterically laughing at her.

"Who do you think you are with this stuck up stuff? And what's so damned funny? I just know what I want and I'm going places in my life. I'm going to graduate, go to law school and marry a millionaire. He is going to be a rich man with values and home training, the kind of man that loves his children and places me on a pedestal. Oh, and he's gonna come home every night. I have never settled for less than what I deserve. That doesn't constitute being stuck up. Your little young ass needs to learn to respect grown people. Your mamma didn't teach you that? Obviously not! "

"Whatever, Little Miss Perfect."

"So......as long as you know. I have a man that wants to marry me right now....see this ring....but I'm leaving without a goodbye....and ask me why."

"Why?"

"Cause he don't know how to treat women and he can't keep his damn hands off me... that's a no no, buddy. So I'm gone and I'm taking this bling with me. He'll learn."

"He probably got insurance on something that big anyway."

"So....I hope he does cause he ain't getting it back...I'm done."

"And let me guess...he is gonna go crazy when he finds out you're gone, right?"

"Good answer.....I guess your Momma did teach you something......I think you need to get back to work now though."

They finally finished the packing and she needed a break more than they did. Her eye sockets were tired of being in surveillance mode. It had been the longest three hours she'd ever known. She was ready for some time alone to say goodbye to her place.

When they finally left, she tried to conjure up memories of her closest friends and the great times they had shared in certain rooms. But she was drawing a blank. She wanted to remember the sensation of signing the initial lease agreement or the excitement in her roommate's voice when they were approved for their application. But nothing registered. Her mind was a huge shell....it was gone...... everything she had suffered was already being deleted from her brain, along with all the good stuff. It felt strange, but her soul admitted to sensing a slight amount of relief. "I should be back to myself in no time."

Though the rude youngster had misinterpreted her with his synopsis of her character and plight, she realized that she hadn't been active enough to contend with anyone about anything since her Mama passed away. She scarcely even had enough power to comb her own nappy head. The apartment had become a dumping station for clothing, tears, and violent screeches into her pillow. The once sought after, Sharon Roberson, found herself routinely barricaded inside for numerous days at a time without any nourishment. Besides this little ordeal and his little antics, her fragile life had been near to feeling like it was finished.

Her little spectator reminded her so much of her crazy baby brother, Terrell, who she also missed immensely. Before her Mama's death, they would go at each other's head for hours, always ending with a hug and a kiss through the phone. Prior to her memorial services, she hadn't seen him since his high school graduation. It was almost immediate that he ran off and joined the U.S. Navy just like their older brother. Along with their father, they enlisted, vowing to serve their great country for a period of time in their lives. But as she pondered over it, she concluded it was mainly for the traveling and meeting new girls....like Father, like son.

Terrell didn't take the news of their Mama's death that well. He received the horrid formal announcement through the Red Cross, who sent for him by emergency procedures; just hours before she left the Earth. That was not the way she thought an individual should hear something of that magnitude. Sharon longed to spend more time with him because she knew he was hurting out there in San Diego, California being all alone. She had been positioned as somewhat of a second mother to him. When he found it difficult to actually talk to their mother about "life", Sharon was easier to share with. He believed her to have more leniencies towards his faults. And now she felt that she had failed him by requiring too much time to herself while ironing out her own personal pain. They always had the gift of making one another laugh, but their

33

laughs had faded as there was nothing humorous about cancer and its ugly face. She did miss laughing, but she missed her Mama all the more, along with him. "I wonder if he'll ever be the same. I know I won't. For now though I'll coin laughter as *good for the soul* like most others do and be amused by the new distraction at hand, him." Sharon found herself indulging in his poor humor because up until the moment he set foot in her apartment, all laughter had been buried with her Mama at her awful departure. Her new acquaintance offered exactly what she had lost.....life. And he came abuse-free. Who would have ever known that they would become so connected in a matter of hours? Who would have known that a teenager would be the answer to her revival? She would definitely talk more with him, perhaps after the game.

Before she knew it, the tournament had progressed and their days of flirting and debating on what being "stuck up" really meant were many. She finally reached the conclusion that that was his adolescent way of saying he'd never met a girl as beautiful and interesting as her before. Her assumption would be decided as correct by their fifth or sixth phone conversation and after returning home from the basketball tournament.

He would call every day of the week and permit her to lay out all of her feelings towards the loss of her Mama, right on the table. She could proceed at any given time, in any given manner, to fret about whatever else in the world was bothering her as well. By the end of the year, he was adopted as her male friend and sole confidant. She never imagined someone that young having the ability to see through the surface of her brokenness and still be able to find something hopeful and radiant inside of her. All this interpretation and insight....with NO SEX....he was everything and more. She could practically tell him anything that was on her mind, her deepest desires and utmost secrets. And he never judged her despite her despair.

His most prominent statement was "You'll make it back and when you do......I'm here. I just know you will because I'm not gonna give up on you. You don't have to rush for nobody....you're hurting right now."

It was her favorite song, possessing a unique melody to it coming from *his* lips. As the months passed, along with the pain, he calls increased in number. His approach was graduating from friend to ....something untamed. He was searching for some progress. She was only looking for an alternate escape route. She tried avoiding him.

But he continued, aggressively he pursued her up until one day, after leaving several messages and running up his grandmother's long distance bill, he says, "Well if you're not going to be *trying* to be my girlfriend, I'm going to have to stop calling you all together. I do love you and so don't get mad. I know you got other stuff to do. But, I can't have my grandmother mad at me for *just a friend*.

But like I said…you can call me because I'm not giving up on you."

It was his first move. "Wow, he left it on the answering machine?" She pressed play and listened to it over and over again. She had memorized it all….every word by the fifth time. She didn't know how to respond though. Though she was very fond of him, she couldn't make sense of the proposal. He had no doubt made her forget about all the cares of this world. With his youth and innocence, he had captured her whole heart and gave it hope again. Not to mention, he could make her laugh until her stomach was twisted into knots. That amounted to something. She needed him to keep doing that. He couldn't possibly stop now……not now, when her sorrow was fading away, with him always on the other line. But there were barriers concerning him. He had *no* money, *no* car, and *no nothing*. "What in the hell am I thinking?"

She had professional basketball players trying to fly her to spend time in Milwaukee; she had professional football players leaving messages with close cousins and friends, waiting for a chance to violate her perfect body. She had music legends worrying her dad for approval on official dates and pricey dinners with them. She had a doctor friend, a bothersome producer….and she was actually contemplating….please. "I can't think about this right now. Besides, I have had a list of dating do's and don'ts thus far:

36

The Dating DON'T List

 1. Don't ever, ever, ever in your whole long life date drug dealers. Just make my own safe money. (And continue to stay alive.)

 2. DO NOT under any circumstances date your brother's friends. (They would kill me, instantly along with the friend...a double homicide? I think not!)

 3. Don't ever date a man with gold teeth. (Everything that glitters ain't really that shiny to me.)

 4. Don't ever even dream of dating a married man. And if he's wedded and absolutely fine... well, think about momma and keep on stepping. (Besides I need my own paperwork and nobody wants to be jump-off...It ain't worth it!)

 5. Don't date broke wannabees. I am going to be financially secure. (I ain't buying you nothing...get your own job!)

 6. Don't date men that don't go to church. (If you don't know Jesus, I don't need to know you!)

 7. Don't date men who beat women (He'd be better off with a crack head...she probably won't mind or even remember after an eight ball or two)

 8. Don't date a man with a small penis (You aren't ruining my night and your reputation. I simply won't be a part of that.)

 9. Don't date men who spend as much time as you do in the mirror? (I don't care how fine he is, he's never gonna be finer than me, I'm the girl...the prize.)

10. Which brings us to the final thought and condition......Don't dare date another woman. I don't share prizes and benefits. We'll be looking for that same thing. (What you got for me, missy, that's gonna make me bow-legged at the end of your sticky little tongue or your unauthentic penile parts?...... nothing........absolutely nothing!)"

37

As she went over her concrete laws again and again, it dawned on her that she had yet to declare any age requirements. She really just didn't know what to do at this point.

"How did I miss that? I need to clear my barely legal little head and get a grip here. Besides, he lives in the country. Who lives in the middle of nowhere? We only see each other once a month and in that time we spend all of it practically blasting the radio as loud as we can, singing songs I don't know *any* of the lyrics to. There is a four and a half year difference in our ages. Why is he trying to destroy what we have? We are phenomenal just like this. I thought we'd be content as friends, forever."

"Hey, did you get my message? You need to check your machine and call me back. I need to get an answer *today*."

"*Today*! Damn, he's bossy. I like that! But why does he have to know *today* and why is he trying to put all this pressure on me? I don't even know if he can kiss. This is moving way too fast. What am I going to say? I like him. His smile affects me on various levels....but a *boyfriend*? Damn! What am I gonna say? Will I lose him forever if I say the wrong thing? His laugh just drives me nuts. Am I falling for him? "

The weekend came sooner than expected and without any prior notice, he borrowed the family station wagon, grabbed his uncle for an alibi, and headed to Memphis.

Before Sharon had a chance to retreat, he was parked in the middle of the driveway outside her Daddy's home, waiting for his answer. She did her absolute best to avoid rendering her decision, because she hadn't really made one.

But he waited while she rambled on and on about how she was seeing other unimportant people and how she was terrified of getting back into a *serious* relationship with anybody, knowing she was unable to give her *all* right now. Then she started running down the complications many of her friends had had while pursuing long distance relationships of their own. She concentrated on how she'd never seen a single one of them work out. As she grasped for straws, she identified a distinctive smirk on his face that made her words come to a complete halt. For the first time since she'd known him, he wasn't even listening to her. It was the blankest stare.

This was the biggest decision she had ever faced in over a year and he had laid this abruptly on her. Now here he was, standing less than three feet away leaning on that ridiculous piece of a car in broad daylight, thinking it's comical to watch *her* attempt to maneuver out of this.....totally unfair!

"I can't believe this!" She could tell by the adjustment in his demeanor though that he now sensed her rage......
"What.....So you find this amusing, huh?"

"No. It's not like that. I've never seen you mad before. You're usually just a crybaby. It's really cute though."

"Whatever. You think it's funny."

"No. What's funny is you and all that *bullshit* that just came out your mouth. I knew you were gonna say that."

"So?"

Then he drops the bomb on her. "So, I already told my mom and dad that I'm going to come live in Memphis for my senior year. You killing me here with the long distance essay though.....now what?"

Damn, he did it like that. She had guessed he told them what to do, too. He had a knack for this bossing thing. She didn't even know what to say. She just stood there in her management uniform, already late for work, and started to cry. After two minutes flat, she realized that there was never another man, young or old in her life that loved her so much that he had to be near her at all costs.

"I don't think I would give up *my* senior year of High School with all *my* childhood friends for anybody."

He was a star athlete, all set to win many of the class favorite statuses. He didn't have many friends in Memphis... how brave. She was overwhelmed by the thought of his apparent sacrifice and of all his advances. He suddenly evolved in her very presence from her closest friend to the most romantic man she had ever known....A man willing to take chances for love. He was a man that wanted something new and real. He had guts, he had

40

height, he had heart and in the sunlight for the very first time, he had some sexy ass brown eyes and a plan!

"Oh, how I love a man with a plan. I am all in now!" Her expression had said it all. He clutched her tighter than ever before, picked her up and twirled her around until she became dizzy. As she basked in his love for her, he proclaimed to all the inquisitive neighbors that he had gotten himself a new girlfriend.

Their hearts entangled as she thought to herself about his run in with her dog and that it was going to be an interesting task making them become friends. She laughed until her cheeks became flushed as he placed her feet once again on the ground. They were official now. She couldn't quite believe it. Though she had never co-signed it, she was fully involved with a younger man that had become part of her very being. He had taken control of their underlined feelings, feelings that she had fought back for months. But now, through his power move and the firsthand security of him being here, perhaps she could let love in again. She could possibly try without the adverse thought off loss, abuse or separation. He was here now…..the only one here from the first step she took to gain control of her life again, besides her Daddy. With one message on her answering machine and one impulsive drive to her home, she was underneath his spell now.

"Okay, baby…..I'm gonna let you get to work. You're already late and I have to get back to Mississippi before dark. My grandma thinks I went to the store. Go get that money. We are going to be needing it for all our dates now....every weekend."

Afterwards he plopped down into the station wagon. It let out a loud screech and he jetted off. She was speechless in the moments that followed. It was truly amazing to her that he would say anything that came into his little head.

"Who tells their girlfriend of two minutes exact that we need your finances to do things? Who just makes someone *into* his girlfriend without an official answer or a real question? And who in the hell plans a long distance relocation to another city, without discussing it with the other person first? This boy is priceless!"

He would just tell her anything and make it their reality. No questions asked, no questions answered, no nothing. Just hey, I got this girl. Do this, girl. It was precisely what she needed, someone in control. He was someone that would tell her exactly what she needed to hear, while obviously believing it himself. Yes, she finally had him here, up and close to her eager ears. And she was anxious to receive every last one of his words.

CHAPTER 2
SECRET LIFE

Sharon had gotten off work a whole forty two minutes later than usual. The ordinary was to have all her part-time associates straighten the racks and pray to Jesus that nobody else wanted to buy male clothing in the store on that particular evening. Being a successful manager definitely had its advantages. The power she possessed had gotten so wicked that if a customer appeared; she carefully chose her words to deter them from purchasing anything, since her register was always pre-counted down several minutes prior to closing. That company was not going to get another ounce out of her. It was an unequal relationship. She had invested all of her time and energy into becoming Manager of the Year and Employee of the Quarter. They had only invested a whopping $1,100 bonus.

"Are you kidding me? Where are all of the incentives you boasted about in the nearly three hour formal interview? I spent more than that on my outfit and shoes that day."

Previously, she was usually on site from dusk to dawn, making sure that every transaction ran smoothly. But the bogus agreement did not seem to be that beneficial to her anymore after laying eyes on that ridiculous bonus check. It appeared somehow to be missing a zero. The lovely Sharon had decided to leave her management position at the Shoe Store for the Men's Store after being fed so many lies about how she would "climb the ladder of success quickly and make *all* the money she had ever imagined."

"Yeah, right........Where are all the zeros then? I log in hours on top of hours." She did have one solid benefit that made her new job seem pleasant at times. It was her perky assistant manager, Shirley Graves. This girl was a handful with her constant need for what Sharon captured as a prescribed medication to keep her calm.

"What else can she take for her condition though? "

The dosage already prescribed was obviously not potent enough for Shirley. She was still bouncing off the walls with energy galore, even after her constant trips to the restroom with the locked door. "But, she surely gets the job done."

Sharon was just waiting for the ideal moment to ask Shirley about her hidden problem. She really wanted to know exactly *what* she was popping and precisely *why*. Drug usage didn't bother her as a manager or a normal person either. Addiction was always a *will* issue to Sharon, never racing to the point of condemnation or being eager to judge others. That's why she was so easy to work with; everyone within the company loved to see her coming. There was no great need for the assistant's secrecy. Sharon had survived way too much to judge.

"Maybe she just needs to meet someone like I did and take a trip to his parents' house like me. Or maybe not.....but I do know one thing......she is making me drowsy just watching her move about. Girl, get yourself somewhere and sit down!"

Nothing could have pleased her more than Shirley's request to leave early in the evening and hinder her ability to close on time.

"Do you think it would be okay?"

"Sure."

She thought she'd never ask. Shirley pretended to have an imaginary phone call, when Sharon was on break. She informed her that there was an *emergency* at her parent's home. But little did she know, Sharon had placed the line in the stockroom off the hook in case the regional manager decided to call and get a recap of the day's events." If she needs to leave that desperately, then she should have just asked." She simply didn't have time for extras tonight; she was too hyped about her trip. So off her little lying assistant went, as she bid her farewell.

"Maybe she is out of drugs. Whatever........She will only be in my way anyways." Her opportunity to close this establishment on time was looking impossible now but she did not fret.

" I am not going to become discouraged because I can do this."

Being in love with Mr. Tell Me Anything had taught her to look at things from a more positive perspective these days. She forbade herself to be in her normal haste and flicked the switch on the sound system, lifting the volume. While bopping to "who let the dogs out," she daydreamed about the weekend and how it would unfold.

Mr. Tell Me Anything was to grab her after work and they were scheduled to travel to his Grandma's house in the country for a weekend getaway. It was their first out of town trip, but it definitely would not be their last. They had grown so close since he moved to Memphis to finish his last year in school. She knew he had missed his buddies and his Grandma so much. Every other sentence for the past couple of weeks was centered on her food or her disciplinary guide that he was much more accustomed to than his new meal plan and stricter curfews. He needed to see her face for a change, so she suggested that they surprise her this evening.

The "country" was the closest they would get to out of town travel. Their funds were now limited because of the many dates and his fetish for hot wings and iced tea. He also was still rapidly growing and Sharon was spending a grip trying to keep him clothed and up to date with the latest fashion in the city. After all.....he didn't reside in Mississippi anymore and Memphians would dare not wear the things that the young folks wore where he was formerly from.....colorful jeans were now out of style. Let the truth be told.....he didn't even own a decent pair of sneakers until they booed up.....unless you consider Pony's to be a proper pair. He had made the sacrifice to be near her so she was totally devoted to becoming his very

47

own personal shopper at her own expense. She didn't mind though, because it was a small price to pay and it would spare her the innuendos being presented from her family. They had depicted him as a young guy that was mooching off of her. Other family members just considered him way too young to discuss. But Sharon only saw him as a striving man that needed more time to become something even more spectacular even if it was a head mechanic and shop owner.

As she thought of their prejudices and the hustle and bustle of managing the store, she could hardly wait for closing time. The trip would be just far away enough for her. It was her very first time staying over at the parent's home of a guy she was dating. She was an absolute nervous wreck.

All of her firsts with him were so remarkable. "He is so amazing. I wonder how the night will turn out."

When previously packing, she had no idea of what to stuff in her overnight bag. "Okay," she thought, "this will be boring enough for her. I will wear these pink pajamas with these white polka dots. They should make me look youthful enough, I believe. "

His grandma was totally opposite of hers. She had plenty of spunk and God knows she did not look her age at all. Sharon worried about what she would think of her. She loved him so much that Sharon could hear it in the tone of her voice, always illuminating through the distant phone lines. She had heard it so clearly the very first time they had ever spoken. He spent hours and hours expressing his deep love and admiration for her. Other than Sharon, she was the only woman he would speak about that she could tell had impacted his life. This was serious......she panicked.

"I *have* to make her like me. Pink polka dot pajamas it is! And what about these thick white socks.....perfect!" She hoped Grandma didn't have super powers like x-ray vision, her grandma sure did. She didn't want her to discover the fire red polish on her pedicured toes, it was a dead giveaway. He loved red polish though. But that wasn't Grandma's business.

Thanks to God, he arrived late for the first time in their whole life together and she was so very elated because she didn't have to keep him waiting as usual. He hated waiting. And just like that, she was leaving the place of non-opportunity, lying assistants and botched benefits. In a flash they were off.

They traveled the long narrow highway, listening to Lenny Williams and laughing all the way. He had known *all* the lyrics to this one classic. It was obviously about a man who really wanted this one woman to know how he deeply loved her. It kind of made her wail up inside as she listened intently. She kept wondering how he knew *all* the words and how in the world did he know that much about love. As for her, well, she pretended to know what he knew. He only sought to see her smile with words coming out of her mouth. They talked, laughed and she faked the lyrics as they got closer and closer to their destination. The rode darkened and narrowed as they approached the small town. She had always been afraid of the dark since childhood, but tonight she felt ultimately safe in his secure company.

As her heart skipped a beat or two, he glanced over at her. "Baby it's cool, we're almost there."

"I'm okay."

The country was further away than she had initially envisioned it. It was taking them forever to arrive. In all her nervousness, she asked him to stop by a local gas station to use the restroom. Without any complaints, he pulled right over and waited patiently for her return to the car.

"How close are we now?"

"Just about two miles down now." He laughed and held her hand, positioning both of them over the middle console. She had his silent promise tonight to never let go. Soon they were there.

"Hey y'all…. come on in here."

"She was so scared because she couldn't see nothing. She ain't used to having *no* street lights."

"Girl, you in the country now. I love it here. I wouldn't move to that city for nothing in the world…..too much going on up there. It's dark but you'll get used to it. Come on inside."

This is where she was wrong instantly. Sharon would never subject herself to such an unpleasant lifestyle overshadowed by darkness every evening. She couldn't even see her hand in front of her face as they had winded in the treacherous curves that night. She had no intentions of *getting used to black darkness*.

But now with the porch light's assistance there was another view for observance. His grandma's front yard was filled with a beautiful garden of assorted potted plants and fragrant rose bushes, all fully bloomed. Sharon could tell right away that this woman had a green thumb. It was a full sky of poised darkness and yet the luminous array of colors glowed into the night being assisted by the Moon's light. It was breathtaking. They were simply gorgeous. She longed for the daylight that would no doubt add to the display of her stupendous night vision.

"My Mama used to grow roses. I hope she doesn't want to talk about growing plants at some point though. I haven't got a clue. I am a *bad* plant mamma. Thus far I've only *killed* anything belonging to the plant and vegetable kingdom. I am actually really pathetic when it comes to gardening. I remember receiving a vibrant potted plant at my mother's funeral. It started out being a deep green hue with a glossy shine on each and every leaf. That thing sent me into a deep depression after it died. I tried, but planting is not one of my better attributes. Who ever heard of overwatering a plant? They waited right until its moment of death to tell me such things as this."

"You have *other* skills that others *don't* have, girl."

"No.....be serious!"

"I am *so* serious."

He was flirting and tugging at the seams of her thongs. It was tantalizing.

Her thoughts and senses were interrupted by the aroma of a scrupulous pot roast coming from inside the house. Sharon knew her food. They entered the three bedroom home with the added on den and she was absolutely, positively correct. Her nose never lied. There it was posted on the stove top, a tender red and juicy roast with thick brown gravy, homemade yellow corn bread, baked sweet potatoes with butter running between the creases, steamed carrots frosted with brown sugar, green beans with chunks of white potatoes thrown in, a fluffy yellow cake with milk chocolate frosting and an oversized jug of chilled bright red Kool-Aid. She loved her already! Grandma and Sharon would be best friends forever.

When they put their bags away they sat right down to eat. She noticed that not a soul paused to say Grace or to wash hands. But she felt too strange about it, so Sharon bowed her head and did her good deed knowing she had washed her own hands previously at the gas station. It felt like God's eyes were on her. Then ready, set, go and they killed that food. She always ate more than the average female, after all, she stood a massive 5'10 inches tall. In actuality, she ate more than the average male, too. You can say she was a tad bit greedy and Grandma noticed as she observed her going back for seconds. She laughed out loud.

"Honey, it's some more in there. I made it all for y'all. I like to see people eat. Eat all you want."

That's all she needed to hear. Her heart was raging along with her enormous appetite. Though captivating, the aroma at Grandma's home was unlike that of her Mama's kitchen. But, it would have to suffice for now. Though they were not her Mama's hazel eyes peeking from underneath her thick lensed glasses, they would have to make due for tonight.

"Oh, how I miss my Mama. The cancer has stolen her and her unique presence from me. I am destined to be an orphan now. It has been decided by God himself that I will face womanhood without guidance now. I need her now. How will I do this without her? It's not fair."

Sharon needed her Mama to tell her the challenges that she was about to face in this "serious" relationship. She had needed to smell *her* pot roast at this moment. She had needed to run to *her* home, *her* kitchen. Her thoughts continued to drift to her childhood when her Mama first taught her to make spaghetti, their favorite family meal. At the tender age of eleven she had fully equipped her with the capability of preparing an entire family meal and believe it.....her brothers had taken full advantage. Even now they called to ask "What did you cook today? "Before they even said hello.

"My God, I miss them too. Has everybody deserted me? Will I ever be complete again? Well, for now I have him and his Grandma and a whole pot roast for comforting." She thought this night would be awkward but she was so comfortable in the kitchen of Grandma's quaint little country home. She wanted a new family to love and cherish.

After dinner she even invited her to lay across the foot of her bed as she pulled out things she brought home from her employer, bragging about how much they loved her. Sharon could see why. She felt like she was staring in a family Saturday special movie. Life was good tonight. And Mr. Tell Me Anything could feel the love as he watched them as they both connected. He loved his Grandma very much and she had seemed more special to him than his own mom. It was important to him that the two women he loved got along well. This was not a problem for Sharon. Grandma was a jewel.

Sharon didn't ask questions about his mom, she just settled into his happiness while adding it to hers. After dinner they cuddled up in the den to watch Jerry Springer. After Mr. Tell Me Anything went off to bed, she was fluffing the pillows on the sofa when Grandma insisted that she go to his room and retire for the evening.

"What? "

Obviously there was some confusion there. She was not your Virgin Mary. Grandma must have had *some* clue. "This is a set up. I just can't do that. We can't be alone like that up in here. This good girl act is not going to last for over five minutes behind closed doors. It's not going to work."

Grandma insisted. She was not taking *no* for an answer. "Girl you better go back there and lay down, you ain't sleeping on no couch."

It was very warm in the house because they didn't have central air. But Sharon was cold natured so she really didn't care. She could hear the floorboards creek underneath her feet and the worn carpet as she tipped down the long hallway quietly to his room. Then, there he was stunned to see her. She imparted to him their entire conversation and he smiled and rolled over to grab her. She was in her man's childhood bedroom in the house where he grew up. It was such an amazing feeling, almost as if she had gone back in time and had been placed into a capsule. She thought of how blessed he was to have a childhood place to return to and a lovely grandma to share it with. With one look at her face, he slid the pink polka dot ensemble off her damp body. She felt complete as he embraced her and shared his life and family with her. It was so amazing to be totally in love on a night such as this. They made quiet love over and over again until he fell asleep underneath her in the heat.

At the break of day, she realized she had forgotten her pill. This was not an issue. The goal was for her to take it as soon as she realized she had missed it. " No problem", she thought.

She had caught it up before in the past without any complications. As she scrambled to locate them in her purse, they were nowhere in sight. Fifteen minutes into her digging, she became very frustrated. Furiously throwing everything onto the bed, she still came up empty handed. Mr. Tell Me Anything questioned her with a tone in his voice she had never heard before. "What are you looking for?"

"My pills."

"Oh, I threw them thangs out of the window at the gas station last night."

"Quit playing."

"No, I'm for real. I've been asking you for over a year about a baby and you keep ignoring me." They were engaged instantly in their first real brawl.

"What the hell are you thinking? Take me home right now!" He didn't even have a job. Sharon didn't care what those scouts were predicting.....that was only a dream at this point.

"Kids can't eat dreams. You can't buy pampers with dreams. I can't believe you would even play games like this. I am not ready to be a mom right now! Take me home!" Sharon demanded that they leave at once. She thought that they had reached a previous agreement....no kids until *she* said so. Now she was jammed up in Mississippi for one more day without her pills.

"That's okay" she thought, "No more sex for him. If I'm miserable, then he's miserable. It's his own fault."

The weekend turned out to be a blast despite his efforts to ruin it and her simple life. She had met several of his childhood friends. They were all warm and kind country boys like people said, really genuine people. Most of them already knew her name by memory; still there was no sign of his mom. Sharon didn't know whether to ask about her or not so she began to do her own private investigation, starting with her brother, his uncle.

All she could drag out of him was that she'd been a beautician and very busy at a young age. He also mentioned there that was an issue that drove him to move in with Grandma. She left it alone. The territory seemed thin to thread on. Still she needed to *at least see her*.

"What in the world are they hiding? Is she a damn crack head? What is the big deal? There's a crack head in just about every family it seems. Who cares? Maybe we can get her some help. This *is* America." Exhausted now, she asked if he had any photo albums and there she was!

57

She looked like the female version of him. She was beautiful! Sharon looked intensely now at the brown skinned little girl in the picture, holding a baby boy that looked like.........*him!* His smooth skin was glowing through the photograph. "That's my baby! She was soooo ..."

"Sixteen" the uncle replied, as though he longed to get the matter out into the universe for her examination.

With the photograph's content, she now understood why he never spoke of her. He was embarrassed. She wondered what happened still. Why did he not live with her? But she decided she would leave it to him to discuss this later. Besides, she had enough problems of her own now with no pills in the vicinity. All she could think of was ending up like the young girl in the picture. Her flattened stomach was her pride and joy. "I ain't giving up my abs for nobody."

At the day's end they returned to Memphis. And after three excruciating weeks of waiting in paranoia, the thing she feared the most had come upon her. Just like the saints of the old had predicted in their scriptures, she missed her period. "Damn, I am doomed."

Her best friend, Kristy Irvin, brought over a home pregnancy test and the stick didn't even turn pink..... it turned bright fuchsia. What in the world was she going to do? Her daddy would kill her. "Oh my God, his daddy is going to *kill* him. What am I going to do?"

They finally discussed their situation after weeks of him enduring her appalling attitude linked to new hormones and thoughts of failure. They had seemed to overpower her true love for him....She was really disappointed in herself. They decided after all the confusion however not to reveal it the pregnancy to anyone. It would be their secret. She would keep this hush-hush under one condition.......

"If anybody asks, especially my Daddy......I am *not* going to lie about it." Sharon was not in the habit of deceiving her Daddy in the past and she wasn't going to start for the pill boy now. She couldn't believe he even asked her to do so. Her dad *hated* when people lied to him.

She somehow managed to avoid her Daddy for the next four months, always working overtime to "save" money. She was going to need all the extra funds that she could get. Every store was filled with baby clothes and baby things. She had no idea what she needed to buy first but she knew that it would be her task alone with his unemployed status. He did however manage to scrape up enough allowances to purchase a small basketball for his "son" claiming that he just knew it was a boy and that he had prayed for him. "Did he pray about my pills, too?"

Sharon almost made it to the fifth month, but his meddlesome father observed her in his driveway one day and decided he'd inquire about her weight gain situation.

"Why is she looking so puffy these days?"

"Oh, she's pregnant, "without any hesitation.

The cat was out of the bag! They had strategically hid their secret, afraid they would both encounter suggestions for abortion and that was *not* an option for them. She really didn't want to be a mother right now but she wasn't going to deny her child the fair right to exist either. She kept fantasizing about whom he'd look like, convinced that she was carrying a son. If it weren't for his father, they could have possibly made it to the labor room. Everyone else had a life of their own and some of *their own* business to attend to. But he was fixated on trying to be a real dad, all of a sudden, in the very last year of his son's school days.

"I just hope that our son has his dad's last name from *day one*....I would hope that he wouldn't wait like his dad to change him into his namesake when his face is plastered all over the newspapers as a local star. I just *had* to see the birth certificate for myself. The image has ruined my respect for him. That *has* to be devastating for my baby....how does he live with knowing that in the back of his mind that he didn't claim him until he got all famous? He just changed his name a couple of years ago. Who does that? Well, surely it is a son that I'm carrying. God wouldn't do us like that. Maybe he will use this baby to show his grandparents how to treat their children....I don't even now but I do know that a girl is not an option. I wonder what his complexion will be. "

Then the scariest thought occurred to Sharon ....
Was he going to be a good dad without being raised by his
father on an everyday basis? Two weeks in the summer
didn't seem sufficient enough to her. Sharon practically
turned her nose up to part-time dads, considering them to
be trifling. She became consumed with this thought. But
with only four months to go, she watched the young dad-
to-be grow into a man that told her everything. He would
tell her of his enormous plans to leave the South and make
oodles of money. He would tell her about his wanting to
make his children proud of him. He would tell her about
his plan to marry her as soon as he possibly could. He
would tell her about his dream wedding. He would tell
her about his fantasies of walking on sandy beaches and
holding hands with her. He would tell her about his
dreams of them owning mansions filled with all seven of
their own children that she was to bare for him. "Okay, not
seven" she thought. "Let's see how we survive this *one*
first."

But he never took *no* for an answer so she wondered
how she would get around that one. She tried to imagine a
house full of kids, but it made her brain ache. What was
she going to do with a house full of children? He would
tell her he'd never loved another woman the way he loved
her. He would tell her she was the most beautiful woman
he'd ever seen in the whole wide world, even better
looking than Halle Berry. (That should have been a dead

giveaway right there) He would tell her his fantasies of playing professional sports. All of his Tell Me Anything stories and dreams were stamped into her heart. She only wanted one thing, to be there every step of the way whether he accomplished it or not. She would be there to hold his hand, one way or the other and now they would have another spectator, their first born....preferably a son.

At the end of her second trimester the ultrasound results were in. She had expected and somewhat spoke into existence what the doctor confirmed. It *was* a boy! When he received the news, he lost his mind. His face was worth a thousand words. He celebrated by putting everybody in their business. She didn't know whether to be upset or happy because he was bragging about it all day. In all the excitement he forgot the biggest obstacle left undone; her Daddy.

After much preparation and discussion and more preparation they headed to his house. They pulled up in the driveway and Mr. Roberson came out to meet them. He had not noticed his daughter's change in weight because she had not seen him face to face in over two more months now. (On purpose) Before her heart stopped pumping, she just blurted it right out. "He's going to tell you I'm pregnant, Daddy."

"And I was going to tell you on my own but he just *had* to tell you first like I couldn't tell you myself. So I'm just telling you….." He didn't utter a mumbling word. He just walked back inside and shut the door behind him. After catching her breath, she rang the doorbell..... No answer.

"Maybe he rushed to pee or something. " She waited, this time she knocked and waited some more. This time he cracked the door.

"What did you need?"

"Nothing, I just wanted to see you..... Talk to you....or"

He shut the door again. She felt like the lowest of lows now. She could perceive his cutting disappointment in her and what she had done. The detestable look had been all over his face, it was worth much more than a thousand words or frown lines. It was more like ten thousand and a necessary facelift. She had been his ultimate pride and joy, always advocating for her every endeavor. And now she laid this whammy on her loving father.

"What kind of daughter am I? How could I allow this to happen on such short notice? He had so many dreams for me and my once promising life."

This pregnancy was far from what he imagined for his baby girl. Often he had fancied her into a lawyer or a prominent woman in the marketing industry of some type; it's what they had planned from the start. Sharon had promised her Mama that she would finish school. This made her somewhat glad that she couldn't see through the door. He was too hurt to lay eyes upon. Refusing to stand there ultimately rejected though....... they left.

Sharon spent the next two days crying her eyes out. "I didn't expect him to be pleased about the news, but I didn't expect him to slam the damn door in my face either. Fine.... I don't need him. I'm going to raise my son myself. Well, we're going to raise *our* son together. Fine."

"Do you want to go eat?"

"No just leave me alone. Look what you did? You think he's happy because I got a baby? You don't have a job. I ain't finished with school. He's scared for me. Damn he looked so hurt."

"What? He don't think I'm good enough? You know that's the issue."

"No stupid, it's always *your* family with all the issues. My Daddy didn't finish law school because he had to work and take care of his three kids. This ain't about you! He's scared for *my* future. Now here I am starring in the repeat episode of his shortcomings in life. Oh my God, what have I done? I'm the stupid one."

"He'll be alright. I'm going to be rich this time next year. Baby I ain't gone let you down. He ain't gonna be able to say nothing. I'm gonna take care of mine."

"Okay, Tell Me Anything. We'll see."

Mr. Roberson relaxed over the next couple of weeks after thinking things through and being challenged by his new wife to be supportive. She was hopeful that the thought of "grandfather" would eventually soften things up a bit. It had such a sophisticated ring to it. He was a classy man so it actually suited him perfectly, if he would just give it a chance.

Just when they thought the coast was clear and time was on their side, he called Mr. Tell Me Anything over for "the man to man talk. "When they both arrived, he was perched on his office chair with a calculator in his hand. "What in the world is his angle here?"

After the men entered the room, Sharon was shut completely out. "What are they doing in there with a calculator?"

The meeting must've gone well because it ended in her Daddy calling her in to apologize. He indicated that he found himself petrified at the thought of his little girl having labor pains of any sort. In their conference, Mr. Roberson had laid out a plan of operation that included what he was offering to provide for his grandchild in life or death. The proposition also outlined what he expected Mr. Tell Me Anything to do once he was capable to pitch in. But his main concern was that his daughter was made to never want for anything in this lifetime. There was not another Daddy like him on this planet! He made her promise to finish school and she did what she learned best from her new baby daddy…. she told him everything he wanted to hear.

They were at peace for now. She could not bear losing him ever. Sharon decided to whisper all the sweet words she knew her father wanted to hear. She didn't need him to give up on her; she had already succeeded in doing that on her own the year before. But now........ She had found someone else to live for, their unborn son.

CHAPTER 3
DRAFTED

"I'm not going to go. Everything thing I've found looks too….. Well….you know how they are."

"So?"

"So you know how those folks are…. they are going to be watching *every little thing* I do. I swear I cannot deal with them this weekend. They already got me pegged as some gold digger or something. I'm so sick of their bull. They are so jealous. It's pitiful. It's like they are all in some rat race to see *who* gets *what* first. I don't want to be part of it."

"No, what's pitiful is that they don't have security in their relationships with him. How do you have a kid and not have a relationship with him or her?"

"Girl, I don't know…All I know is that I'm so sick of it….they all just need to sit down and talk and quit dragging me into the drama. I ain't got nothing to do with her abusing her kids and him neglecting his. Even Mr. Tell Me Anything should let it go….that was so long ago. If I was headed to make that kind of money I would forgive everyone and wish them the best. Their greedy behinds would get one big fat check each and a goodbye speech to go along with it until we all get together to sing Christmas Carols and stuff…….but he just keeps holding the crap over their heads…..Damn….let it go. It's really ruining our life. He's mad at them and the world *all the time*."

Kristy Irvin was shopping with Sharon her for the perfect outfit. The occasion was the start of the new phase of her perfect life together with her perfect Mr. Tell Me Anything. She was closer than ever to getting away from them, the largest group of meddlesome unemployed grown people ever known to mankind. Even the men quit their jobs with his new career underway.

Kristy had always been very supportive, the two being joined at the hip through a lifelong friendship because of their mothers' bond. Ms. Irvin had filled in on many nights after Sharon's mom had passed away. They both wanted the best for her. But this day would prove to be more than a shopping event; it would be an opportunity to vent for Sharon and for Kristy to lie to her as usual about how skinny she was and how she could possibly make it through the upcoming events.

"Girl, but he looks so happy right now. You have to go. He would die without you, crumble. Forget about them folks. You look too good not to go!"

"See, that's why I brought you with me, you're so right. Okay, but the first sign of drama and I'm out of there. I'm not going to let them keep up their crap about me. It's about to be his big day that he's been waiting for all his life. Nobody is going to use their bad thoughts about me to bring him down. I promise..... They are not going to spoil this for him with their bull."

Sharon needed this dress to be perfect for her budget and her body. He had just ordered a custom suit that they had to scrape up the money to buy. Their new budget consisted of 80% of her salary and 20% of donations from her family. To make matters a little more tight, the tailor measured their son as well. They had no intentions of leaving him out. The order was placed; they selected matching three piece custom tailored black and white pinstriped suits. She thought that she was going to pass out when they arrived along with the final bill. But nevertheless, it was worth it. Besides, she was used to taking care of all of them now.

He had opened the box with much anticipation. Then he slid his slender body into the ensemble. There they were, her two men with matching names and matching suits. They were about to embark on making their name great in the world of sports. It was a dream waiting to come true and a small price to pay for it.

"So what are you going to wear if you don't wear that?"

"I don't know but it's definitely got to be black. He wants me to match him and the baby. He insisted on something black. But I do love this one. I'm just more worried about my hair than anything else. I've wanted to cut it."

She always cut or dyed her hair when her nerves got bad. But this time he was totally against it saying most ball players had women with long hair and big tits. The tit part she already had covered with breastfeeding and growing a whole cup size, though she was not opposed to implants if necessary.

"Maybe later," she thought to herself. If she laid out for the next two days she could possible add some color to her fair skin for the weekends' events and appear Brazilian or exotic. It was the Month of June. She hadn't basked out in the sun the entire season. She was way too busy working overtime saving enough money for the planned days approaching. They needed money for clothing, extras, possible shopping and for haircuts, salon appointments, manicures, pedicures, teeth whitening, you name it. So she worked her little ass off. All Sharon could think about was that this big day was going to be televised. Everyone would see them for the first time together nationwide. It would be broadcasted in every common and uncommon household. They both could hardly wait. And her credit cards couldn't either. They were stretched to the max. By the end of the day she had found it...

"Perfect.........What do you think about this one?"

"He won't be able to focus with you looking so good, girl." Kristy had made her decision for her.

"Yes....."

"Other than the birth of our son and being named sophomore of the year in the sports world, this is the biggest thing that's ever happened to him."

"No, silly.....you are!"

71

As the days went by and her savings fund decreased in size she had to maintain her composure. He needed her financial support and strength to rely on. This was no time to bail on him. As he kept practicing his acceptance speech, she was forced daily to be attentive, with disturbing thoughts of her new found growing debt lingering in her head.

"So how does that sound? Do I sound stupid?" His voice wasn't sounding ludicrous at all. The employment acceptance speech was delivered to her as glorious because she had been the only one with a job for the past five years. She was actually thinking that maybe he should shorten it a bit and get on with receiving the paychecks.

"How much do they pay anyway?"

"Quit playing, girl. I'm gone keep doing it until you feel it."

"I already feel it....*you* need to feel it." Sharon often told him that he looked nervous and that she didn't understand why. He was always on television doing interviews in college. He was practically the face of his team and a very well-spoken specimen of a man.

"Why are you so scared now? He was starting to frighten the life out of her. "Do you know something that I don't know?"

She really didn't comprehend it all until they actually reached their destination, the Big Apple. There were cameras everywhere! From the time their plane landed, there were news teams and reporters following them and the others around speculating over who would go where and in what order. It was enough to make a person go mad. It was actually enough to make him abandon every single word he had practiced. "Oh my God, what is he going to do?"

He kept spying at her with that *look* the entire weekend. It was a survey of needing her strength to keep his head right. "He is the *star* so why in the hell is he looking at *me*?" Wait a minute. She started feeling the pressure that he was undergoing; it was too much for them both. So, she finally persuaded him to disappear for a while to a remote location, where she would soothe the both of their toxic nerves with a little sex therapy, all hands free, they were both fine now. He reappeared with the tranquility she needed him to have. She resurfaced with swollen lips and with what felt like a hole in the back of her throat. Now it was his turn to turn the heat up.

"I wish they'd get on with this." She had a habit of being a tad bit impatient. Sharon really wanted to see the order he would be called in. Though his body was calm now, her mind was yet racing with multiple thoughts. She worried whether he would remember his speech. She wondered how much time they would be allotted to find a house.

"Am I going to get lost trying to find my way around the city? I have no sense of direction. Who's going to stay with me when he's on the road? Do the other wives or girlfriends do stuff together? Do they give us free tickets for our family? Is he going to be the same? Is this money stuff going to change him?"

She looked over at him, her nerves rested again. There he was, her baby. Despite everything ….. he was her baby. She loved him. He loved her. Even a child could see it. They would be fine. Whatever came their way, they could make it through. "Why am I tripping?"

She guessed he could see the concern on her face because he drew very close to her and kissed her tired lips. After her mind returned to its natural state, he gripped her hand firmly with his sweaty palm. He began to squeeze harder because she needed to respond to a reporter who asked if she was excited. She kept it short and sweet, looked right into the camera with her charming enhanced smile and replied, "Yes, very." Only two words and he was taken by her temporary enlarged lips.

"My God….. You guys make an awesome couple." The reporter was astonished at them. This statement was the start of their stardom life together. They had made their public debut now.

Afterwards, they scurried over to the hotel where family members tried to pry him away immediately mentioning a pow-wow in the parent's room where Sharon wasn't invited. The discussion was rumored to be centered around his dad's delusions. According to several members, his dad informed the family, in this assembly, about his views towards a certain "illegitimate child" that would taint his son's image if he were seated at the main table.

After returning from their meeting, the news was delivered by Mr. Tell Me Anything in a manner that spoke of disgust and a terrible dishonor. Sharon wanted to head for the nearest airport. The matter jostled her into a position where she found herself warring in battle on the very first day of their arrival.

"I can't believe this bullshit. He had the nerve to say he was only trying to *protect* my image."

But all Mr. Tell Me Anything heard on that night was that he didn't want his only son at the table and he had not wanted him to exist, publicly. Just as Sharon had decided to push the forgiveness slogan...he blew it! She now decided to back off and let the chips fall wherever they fell.

They were both devastated. Their son meant the world to him. They wanted to take everything he loved away from him. He had already dealt with speculation surrounding paternity because their son was born with blue eyes and pale skin like Sharon's grandfather, but now this.

"This is too much. These people don't quit. All of a sudden, on the *very first day*, he is trying to shut the gate on us..........He's hideous...."

In a moment, Sharon figured out his father's process of thinking. He had no doubt believed that if they sent the baby from the table she would follow, tucking her tail in the process. "No way buddy!" She arched her back, stuck out her chest like her Mama taught her. With her sword embedded in her vocal cords she spoke in the most dignified voice. "Let's just keep the peace. He will sit with your brother and the other family up in the risers and I will stay with you, baby. There are lots of important people seated up there. Don't worry it may be better this way. What if he decides to cry too much or cut up? You know he can't sit still for too long. Don't worry, stay focused."

She swallowed her pride but inwardly she was furious and highly insulted, knowing they had already gotten off to a good start with their bull. Trying to screw her over had become an art for these people. And the father was the ringleader. This was going to be a part time job for her if they didn't hurry and get things under control.

"Where is the love?" She thought. At this point his mother had hired herself as his personal informant, always forthcoming with poisoned gossip. She felt it necessary to exaggerate the schemes of others in an effort to "manipulate the situation" and show her new depths of loyalty towards Mr. Tell Me Anything. It was like watching the horses at a race. Sharon sat back, cautiously observing and she put all her money on herself. She knew where she stood. Nothing was going to tear them apart.

"How do these people *not* get that part? He is mine. We are a team and anyone who opposes us is an opponent. This is his day and this is his dream." With all the circumstances surrounding their son, she was going to stay in defense mode as long as necessary, but try to enjoy the moment with him. "Nobody is going to run over us, nobody! And nobody is going to ruin his day, nobody!"

After the fiasco at the hotel they retired to their room where he poured out his precious heart to her. It was one of the most intimate conversations they had had in their life together. He began to speak about his childhood and how he wanted to provide for his Grandmother. He told her that he wanted most of all to make his parents proud so they could love him the way he desired. It was saddening to hear that because she had parents that were quite different than his, they loved her severely *for free*. It was way too much at times for her to grasp. She was raised with the both of her folks in holy matrimony. After being married a couple of years, her Daddy had purchased their family home when she was born on the account of her very existence. He didn't want his only baby girl growing up in an apartment without a backyard to play in. They had lived there together until her senior year of High School when they divorced after several family discussions. Her people were obviously knitted a little more closely together than his but she didn't like judging people so she tuned back in to his voice.

Mr. Tell Me Anything expressed himself thoroughly. He said that he always wanted to know why they didn't even try to be together. It troubled him how so many people had babies if they weren't in love with the other person. He thought it to be a stupid act of selfishness. He concluded that single parenting ruined lives.

"Not his and not tomorrow," she thought. "Tomorrow he will rise above every bad thought and every day he missed having his father and mother together and he will shine. He will make them proud as he wishes. He will be rich and they will love him like never before."

Sharon didn't really understand how money would restore things that were absent over a period of several years. But she did understand this one thing, if they kept on messing with her and *her* baby, there was going to be trouble. She decided in that moment that she would love him and protect him at all costs. He needed her. She looked him deeply into his eyes and told him what he wanted to hear.

"I love you baby and I will always be here. Remember, you are going to be very happy. You have been there for me all this time.....I will never leave you." Then they curled up and their love for one another sent them into the most peaceful sleep.

The next day would start a little too early for her. The sun was beaming through the opened shears and their son was beating on the window seal, whining from hunger. He practically never got full. Fortunately, his Grandmother came to the rescue. In a matter of moments he was taken to her room and the couple was alone once again. This time they didn't say a word to one another. She had never seen him without words before. Bewildered by his demeanor, she had to speak. "You okay baby?"

"Yeah, just thinking."

"About what baby?"

"About where we gonna live and about you."

"What about me?"

"Nothing, just, I can't live without you and I know you don't want to leave your family but I'm not going to leave you in Memphis. I don't care what my family says."

"Are they saying I should stay home, too?"

"Baby, don't get mad, this shit is already getting stupid. Hell, we been living together all this time. And they think I'm going to leave y'all in Memphis. This shit is crazy. I hate them!"

"Look baby, today is your day. Take that back. You really have got to let that stuff go. Ain't nobody keeping us away from you. Tonight you are going to be a freaking millionaire. You shouldn't be thinking about me, our son, your mother, your daddy, Tom, Dick, Harry, Sally or Sue.

Do you understand what I'm saying baby? You have worked your ass off for this. When everybody else was still in bed sleeping, you were running around that damned lake and missing all the movies on Friday nights and all the other stuff young dudes get to do in High School. In college, you had a freaking curfew. Boy I was dancing on tables in the club all night till the sun came up when I was that age. You deserve this more than anyone I could ever imagine. Don't let their bull get in your head. You are a star....they want you. You are the elite of the elite right now. Forget about them and their new found laws. Be proud. You're going to be a freaking millionaire in a couple of hours. Quit letting them get in your head. Tonight is your night."

"A freaking millionaire!" He said it again, "A freaking millionaire!"

Then he snatched her up on the bed and they started jumping up and down with a celebratory dance. He had to bend his back over in order to avoid getting knocked out by the ceiling. It was the best moment they had since that damn plane landed. They started screaming out of the windows at the passing cars and strangers.

"I'm rich bitch, I'm rich bitch!" The couple fell to the floor gagging.

"See baby, be happy. You're a rich bitch now."

Then they gagged again. Damn she loved him. To top it off, he was gonna be her rich ass, fine ass boyfriend/baby daddy in a matter of hours. She couldn't believe it! They were best friends, who fell in love. She struggled to provide for him and their son, but now he could finally pay a bill!

"Yes lord, he can pay a bill now. Thank you Jesus!"

Then he fell to the floor again and said, "Yeah baby, call your boss and tell him I'm rich bitch. It's a wrap."

She pretended to take his words lightly but she was giving unemployment some serious thought now.

"What if he started tripping after I quit my job, then what? What if I moved and had one of my spoiled fits and he put my ass out, then what? What if his family convinced him after all their bullshit I wasn't right for him, then what?"

The questions kept flooding in. She had heard that professional athletes were all wayward and that their families did nothing but battle over their fortune with constant interference forever. "Is it true? "

Now they had their share of contempt with his dad's new seating chart. She believed the concept was that you were only allowed a certain amount of people at the main table as a player. And they were already counting them out.

"So soon? Damn! What kind of mess is this? Honey, this is a time when you've got to be a grown ass woman." So here goes, "Baby did you figure out *who* was going to sit *where* at the table tonight?"

"Yes, you and so and so and so and so and so and so."

All she needed to hear was her name first. He was off the hook now. All secure, all the others faded into the background where they belonged. She didn't hear anything after that. She didn't know who or what or when, she was still captivated by her son, in his matching suit, being transported to the high risers.

"What the hell, I'm not going to lower myself to their standards. He loves the fact that I'm a bit stuck up. He's said that even from our first meeting. He loves this educated woman with this strong backbone. To him, my vocabulary has been extraordinary, being a speech pathology major of two years. Tonight, I will dig deep into my elaborate database to simply conceal my thoughts. I will keep my words short and sweet for him. He doesn't need the entire extra thing right now. I will straighten my back as a vow to my mother and for my innocent son I will fight silently, until further notice."

The hours passed by at lightning speed. They entered the room full of bright lights, rolling cameras, and action! She could hear his name ring in the mouths of everyone in the building. The injury sustained to his foot prior to the event was the main topic. Many thought it would decrease his ranking and his stock. Others thought his height and resume would speak for themselves. He was a known defender and rebounder. But, she didn't have any thoughts about rankings, stock or height because her thoughts were centered on keeping peace at the table for him.

The family was already into somewhat of an uproar. Evidently, the stepmom had been accused of wearing a newly purchased ring at the expense of Mr. Tell Me Anything. It wasn't all that extravagant of anything to look at in Sharon's opinion, but the family was aggravated because they suspected some major money had already exchanged hands without their knowledge. As the argument escalated, the stepmom went to the restroom where Grandma would follow to interrogate her. She proclaimed it was costume jewelry only. In unbelief, the grandmother began to raise her voice.

"Well cut the glass, cut the glass, let's see if it's fake."

What a disaster! But Sharon had to admit, Grandma kept her rolling on the entire trip and she loved her tenacity. She definitely was a force to be reckoned with, so wise in her full protection mode. In that moment she was glad that they were allies.

"She's not the kind of woman you want to draw battle lines with. "

Her motives seemed quite different than any of the others'. In Sharon's opinion, she was more like her, the one he could depend on, the one who had his back the whole way through when others had beaten and abandoned him. She was the one there. She was the one who had bought his three owned outfits when they met from Penny's with her card. He had called her his "favorite" and for that she would remain Sharon's also. As the drama unfolded she suggested that they all stay calm and return to the table. She wasn't gonna let these morons make her miss another moment. He hated when she was out of his sight.

"Where have you been? What was taking so long? I can't breathe out here. Don't leave me again. I need to look at you so I won't be nervous. Damn baby I'm nervous. Why haven't they called me yet? Where have you been?"

She turned to him, grabbed his gorgeous bronzed chiseled face with both hands now adorned with fresh French tips and kissed him smack on his lips.

"You are gonna be fine. You're next. Just wait and see."

She wanted to give him a nastier kiss but her lips were still recovering from their earlier activities and she didn't want to smudge her perfect lipstick. She was going to be on national television in just a moment. Her peck seemed to console him as he held her hand underneath the table where no one could see. He didn't let it go either until he had gotten so anxious again that he needed to retreat to the men's room.

Sharon watched the other players being called as predicted while he was absent from the table. She could read the announcer's lips as they approached other tables searching for theirs. Every table was labeled with the players name on an ornate centerpiece. So, she positioned the plates and other items out of the way to make his tag more visible. Finally, they spotted him making his way back through the crowd.

"Where were you? Baby, here they come."

"It's my turn?"

"Yes, sit down and look surprised."

She began to cry and smile. It was an awkward expression but she couldn't help it. She was overjoyed and very proud of him at the same time. Then she was also scared to death for him and irritated by the lack of class they had expressed in the restroom full of other spectators. He was about to be prompted to deliver the biggest speech of his life, while he just had some of his closest family members scrapping in the bathroom over money that he hadn't even earned yet. His wealth had already begun to create a war zone.

"Do I really want to be a part of this? " First she thought, "Hell Yeah! I want it." Then she looked around the table and there they were, the Family.

There were only two smiles; the rest of them she gathered had built-in calculators modifying numbers in their heads. Perhaps they were adding and adding but Sharon was only subtracting their little ghetto fabulous, money hungry behinds right out of the new equation.

And one thing she knew for sure......... she was ready for whatever.

"They say only the *strong survive*. Somebody better tell them what's up!"

CHAPTER 4
THE TRAIN WRECK

"Hello"

"Hello is Mr. Tell Me Anything there?" (pause)

"Surely this must be the wrong hotel room. I will definitely call back." Sharon had been calling his room for over two hours now with no response. She hung up.

It had been an unwelcomed challenge seeing that she had to steal the hotel information from the wife of another teammate, Carmella Murphy. She pretended all the while that Mr. Tell Me Anything had already given it to her and that she had somehow misplaced it. She spent seven whole minutes scheming up on how to ask for the number without appearing suspicious or unworthy of having it. Mrs. Murphy had become her idol over the past couple of months, always parading into the games in California with her Louis Vuitton and Chanel collectibles. She was a very attractive woman who commanded the attention of the crowd. Sharon vowed to learn all her techniques.

Because they weren't quite married yet and she was just a fan, Sharon didn't want to jeopardize anything with juvenile behavior patterns, she wanted to fit in. She had to use her head here. So she got her tattered nerves together, put on her most educated and concerned voice, while Mrs. Murphy spilled the beans willingly. It was almost as if she already knew what Sharon was up to. She had heard that there was a code for athletes' wives. Unsure of what that really was, she still desperately needed to get the information in a timely manner. To her surprise, she had extended an open invitation telling Sharon to "please call if you need anything else." She had made progress in her venture to "fit in" with the Diva world. Her life was coming together so quickly that it scared her.

Sharon placed the call again deciding that this definitely had to be the wrong room.

"Guest services"

She tried again. "May I please have the room of Mr. Tell Me Anything?"

"One moment mam while I connect you."

"She better get it right this time. These people need more competent workers. I'm gonna have to report her. "

This time she answered with an attitude, "Hello, who is this?"

Did this heifer just ask me, the wife-to-be, who is this? "Honey, who is *this* and let me speak to Mr. Tell Me Anything?"

"Is this Ms. Roberson?"

It suddenly occurred to Sharon that the female knew her name. She snatched back the sheets of her luxurious silk fine linens as she started her fifty questions, with her game face on. As she reached the edge of the California King bed, Sharon fell into the most awkward position and started drilling her ass.

"So who are *you* and how do you know *me* and where is *he* and why are *you* answering *his* phone?" Did he trust this strange female enough to have her in his unoccupied room with his personal belongings lying around? Was he lying there beside her just allowing her voice and her presence to smash her heart into itty bitty pieces? Was he in the shower while this stranger was taking two minutes to destroy his already planned out life with her vicious words? This great big fantasy was filled with Sharon (not her) making all of his dreams come true. It was planned right down to the expected childbirth of five more children. Was this girl crazy? They had just purchased their very first home. It wasn't a mansion but six thousand square feet is huge in Los Angeles California for two adults and two small children. Yes, they had a son and a newborn daughter. She had been proposed to and was peeling through the next two months to become his beloved on paper. The stage had already been set. He himself had done *all* the planning. He had paid all the fees up front and met with the coordinator in an effort to prove his enthusiasm that seemed quite convincing. He had done such a terrific job that she was beginning to feel left out. She often blushed as the coordinator would say; "I've never seen a man *this ready* to get married before. Girl you are so lucky to have him."

No one could tell her anything different than that. She was reminded of his reinforced love and dedication every day with the constant glare of her newly purchased five karat round diamond engagement ring. Carmella Murphy herself had met him at the jewelers to offer ideas of its design. He paid well over fifty grand for that thing. Oh, that was just the weight of the center stone because the band itself weighed in at well over three additional karats...... How he loved her! Sharon was a heavy weight now.

Mr. Tell Me Anything had proposed in a limousine headed to dinner one night in Miami Florida. They left their newborn daughter behind because he had insisted that it was Mother's day and he needed one whole day to spend with her and show her just how special she was to him. She should have known. As they began to ride around and observe the bright city lights, he got down on one knee in the limo and said, "I am the last boyfriend that you will ever have and you are the last girlfriend that I'll ever have. Baby will you marry me?"

"Then he begin going on and on about how I meant the world to him and all this Bull! Who in the hell is this female on the phone then? .... "She gathered her composure "Look, I don't mean to be rude but explain to me why you are in my fiancé's hotel room? Yes, we are getting married in two months."

"Oh my God, he told me that you guys weren't together anymore, just real close friends. So you don't live in San Diego with your brother and the kids?"

"Honey, hell naw, I live in our house with my name on it. I sleep in our bed, with his scent in it. He lives with us every day of his life. It's me and our two kids and him.

91

And he's going to *keep* living with us so you need to get your raggedy ass out of my man's room and recognize that you are just a jump-off, a stupid one at that."

Click, Click. "Did this heifer just hang up on me…Awe, hell naw! "

"Ring, ring ring ring ring", no answer. "Ring ring ring ring ring," no answer. "Oh, she's gonna answer this phone because I'm not going to let her swipe his personal belongings while he's passed out in his friend's room or something."

She had drugged him. It must be the reason she hadn't heard from him. "He's somewhere unconscious. I saw this once before in a movie. She knew my brother lived in San Diego, how? Yeah, that's right; he was always talking about me. This slut was a friend of a friend, no doubt. Some talkative teammate has given her all this free information about me. Besides, she is the one concerned about me; all I am concerned about is this rock on my finger and my limo proposal."

Sharon was at *their* house, in *their* bed, with *their* children. This phone girl was nobody. "He loves me. I'm not going to let this little tramp stand in between our destined future."

They had dated six whole years prior to his proposal. Surely there was time enough for him to make a good sound decision. She didn't ask *him* to marry *her*.

She needed time to deliberate so she waited for fifteen minutes. She decided to call back again. This time she allowed the phone to ring twice. Ring. Ring. "Hello."

"Hello, is that you?"

"Yeah, hey baby, I was sleeping, I'll hit you back when I get up."

"Naw, you ain't been sleep, I just spent the last twenty minutes talking to yo bitch and you better not hang this phone up because I want to hear you tell the jump-off to get out. Tell her right now. I ain't playing with you! I can't believe you, what are you thinking? Why is she there? Why did you tell her that I lived with my brother? What are you doing? So all this time you're planning all this bullshit with the coordinator and this is how you gonna do it? You better hope you can get your $40,000 back because I'm done. And I don't want to hear from you.........I'm gone. "Click!

Ring. Ring. Ring........."Baby calm down, this bitch" she listened as he spoke, "rode the train down here from Boston. I'm minding my own business and she shows up saying she ain't got no money to get back home. So I let her chill here until her cousin got ready. She is actually down here with another player. Baby please calm down. Bitch, you need to roll."

She tries to speak, "But you told me" and then he interrupts, "I ain't told you shit. Get the hell up out of here, don't you see you're upsetting my wife."

Sharon could hear the door slam behind her. "Tell that bitch like it is baby! " He had never called her his wife before. See she had just received the ring eight months ago and they had not had the actual ceremony. "Mrs. Tell Me Anything". It rang so loud in her head that she had forgotten that her husband-to-be had an out of town roommate for a night. It rang so loud in her head that she had forgotten that he had partied until 4:20 a.m. and successfully managed not to answer his cell phone all night. When she came back to earth and her bare senses, she began the questioning again.

"So, where the hell were you all night and all this morning?"

"Oh, I stayed in my partner's room because I didn't want to be bothered with that bitch. She was all pitiful, trying to make me feel sorry for her, begging ass. Baby I'm glad I got you. These girls out here are something else."

It was just what she wanted to hear. So, there you have it, she was the beggar and Sharon was the soon to be bride. "Well, too bad for all you groupies. I am the one and only," she thought.

"Women are so pitiful when they prey on something that belongs to someone else. Newsflash, you ain't having mine. "Sharon began laughing inside hysterically and outwardly smiling as if she had hit the lottery. She was covered with a sense of "I won this time" kind of pride. He was such a prize. He stood a few inches short of seven feet tall. He was tall, dark and handsome was not the word because he was much more than that. This man, her man, was gorgeous. He had one of the most perfect set of teeth a person could ever have and possessed the nicest ass and the biggest package she had seen in all her years.

On their first date he looked at her so seriously that she questioned him as to why and he told her, "Girl, I'm going to marry you and you're gonna have all my babies."

Sharon had laughed to herself. She thought of him as a baby himself. She thought of his unemployment. Then she thought of her own age and the things she had left to accomplish. Besides, she was afraid of stretch marks and hanging guts. There was no way that she was going to lose her figure or hang an infant from her breast. But she was all that he had asked for now with two little ones on deck. He should have left the kids out of the equation.

"I might have to shoot myself in the head for sure. "

"So, why didn't I hear from you last night? Your friends have phones in their rooms and you have a cell phone. I'm not trying to hear this! Please don't lie to me because I can go home. I got a daddy and my own damn house. I don't need anybody lying to me. You can pay your child support and get your money back for this wedding because I ain't got to marry your cheating ass.

"Baby, please! I'm gonna call you from his room and I'll let him tell you where I was."

"Oh no, then they will know that we are having problems. Are you trying to make me look totally insecure....So you wanna spread this stuff to all of the other wives? I'm already the one with the two prior kids who just got a ring. So no! You are not gonna let your damn teammate destroy my reputation. I have worked too hard for this. Screw you and her." Click.

Ring. Ring. Ring. "So you hate me now?"

"No...I'm just gonna let you get back to your *road* life." Click.

Ring. Ring. Ring. "Baby."

"What!"

"Baby....I would not do that to you. It's just us two in this."

"It's okay, I believe you but let's just stay on the phone a while since she's gone. She is gone right?"

"Yeah baby that bitch *been* gone. I had no contact with her. I love *you*. We can stay on this joint all night. Let's sleep with the speaker on...alright?" The problem lied in the next question which was the same question as before,

"So, how did she get there?" Normally he had a one track mind with a span of about four to five minutes. She knew if there was some type of discrepancy now would be the time to discover it.

"She flew down or something with her cousin." Sharon remembered that he specifically said that she had ridden the train from Boston. He was hiding something, definitely he was hiding something and she needed to know what.

"I thought she rode the train."

"Awe yea, baby what difference does it make?"

"Just answer the damn question. Every time you lie, just tell the same lie. Don't play with me!"

They went back and forth for over an hour until she was mentally drained. She gave. She wanted to be with him and she couldn't see herself starting over with his two babies and no career, an unfinished education, with unfulfilled dreams for some stupid bitch and these half ass answers, so she gave in. She decided to keep a close eye on him instead. She would be blowing up his phone from now on. She wouldn't sleep when he was on the road. She would call his ass until he became so miserable and he would *never* try this again. "Besides, what could he say? He did this. Who lets a strange woman into their hotel room when they're getting ready to be married to me? Don't worry; I got this all under control. "

"Hello, Baby, are you feeling better now and are you still the love of my life and getting ready to be my wife?"

There he was again with the "wife" thing. It was all for nothing. The man had her at "hello." He had cared enough to call right back when his coaches said no more phone calls tonight. He had broken the rules for her once again, putting it all on the line. She was special to him indeed. Her man loved her and it was nothing he wouldn't do to prove it. So he begged as the plane ascended into the air. He never hung up......just held the line until the airwaves had cancelled the call. He was on his way home.

"She better jump her ass on that train and forget she ever knew anything about him. He is all mine, all mine and come hell or high water.........I am going to take those vows in two months with the man of my dreams. Things aren't always as they seem."

Sharon vowed never to let another outsider upset her again. Then she drifted asleep with the melody of wedding bells ringing and hints of soft kisses to come.

CHAPTER 5
STACKED

It was late. Well, it was not very late, but late enough. It seemed as though she was running out of time. She had just barbecued for the evening to come when some of Mr. Tell Me Anything's family would soon get to sample her goods. It was her first opportunity to show them what she could do on the grill. How was she going to get them to love her food when they despised her? Tomorrow she would have her one slim chance.

Her fiancé's father was "okay" with the idea of them living together now, because he didn't seem too thrilled about the fact that she had already conceived two children who were very deserving of child support payments. He was very protective of Mr. Tell Me Anything's newly found fortune, almost as if it was partially his. To make matters worse, he officially relocated to Los Angeles along with his entire family. He was sure to follow the money trail. The couple was totally embarrassed by his power move.....it seemed so desperate on his behalf. Nobody else had had their parents follow them around.

The other players normally had the opportunity to fly their parents in to stay for a weekend and catch a great game or two....but not *actually move* to where they were.

Her man was a man of stature now, reeling in a whopping five million dollar contract. But Sharon felt sorry for him. He was the laughing stock of all his team. While he was chasing his son's money, he had ruined his image, alone. There was no coming back from the damage he had done. It made him feel small minded and untrustworthy.

"So, I can't take care of myself when I *have* money but I can when my aunt has to steal coats out of stores to keep me warm my whole life?"

"Baby, just let it go.....that was a long time ago. Just tell him how you feel and send him home. Besides, you ain't stolen a coat in six years. "She tried to provide a sense of humor but it was not registering. Her man had the gift of selective hearing. His hatred for them at times was overwhelming. She had wished it several times into the sea of forgiveness where God had sent her wrongs. But he could not grasp the concept. It was festering inside his young soul.

But when he was among the public, he was quite a different creature. Often he exuded a confidence unfound by others. It was so enchanting to watch him make grand entrances and see all the female's eyes light up with dreams of giving mad blow jobs that would make him fall in love with them. But little did they know, Sharon already had that area under control and that he was one shake away from break! Sharon was giving her man everything she had and still there was a unique void. He still needed her though. And she needed him as well.

Due to his unfortunate childhood, he had tons of responsibility at such a young age. With a mother who had recently died after suffering from breast cancer, she had her share of young responsibility as well. Too much had happened to the both of them and they grew up way too fast. Their huge deficits made them fully connected. They sought desperately to fill their emptiness with each other. Whatever else they were to encounter they had decided to do it together with all others on the outside of their circle, or at least that's what she thought.

Sharon had attended at least four of his professional games now. Shortly afterwards, she was informed by other wives/significant others that this one particular female was spreading numerous lies about herself and her Mr. Tell Me Anything. They would ramble on and on about how he was supposedly banging her providing lots of explicit details. So, she listened as carefully as she could until one night she became fed up with the vicious gossip.

"You guys are really crazy. Have you seen her teeth?"

She had too many of them in her mouth. She had layers and layers of discolored permanent teeth in that mouth of hers. To add to her apparent flaws and misfortune she had the kind of acne that needed immediate attention, the type that over the counter medication could not begin to cure. She tried to conceal this catastrophe with pounds and pounds of foundation, but she had had little success. The miles of bumps on that face were protruding right through, what a hot mess!

"You got it all wrong. Girl y'all can't believe everything you hear. You guys just let anybody come in and wreck shop. I've seen gold diggers his whole college career. These girls be out here lying and hating and wishing."

"Girl, you just in love. That damn girl ain't lying about *everything*. And remember to every lie there *is some* truth. You need to wake up."

"Naw, y'all just be looking for stuff. That's why y'all got all these problems at home. We don't have those kinds of problems. Y'all just paranoid."

She had to totally convince them along with herself. Besides, she wasn't quite prepared for the paranoia associated with having a star as a husband. She had needed more time to think about this before she made it official. And she was in the middle of planning her wedding. She already had the ring and she could possibly get away with keeping it without actually doing the *thing* if the accusations became a reality. She already had one failed engagement ring on deck. Maybe she would become a collector. She would argue that it was a consolation prize for all her years of service and for dealing with that damn family of his. Or maybe she would find this crap to be true and bail. She needed more time to figure this thing out. All of the details had seemed so real coming from their mouths. They had no real reason to discredit him. But none of them trusted any of their own husbands.

Even it wasn't true, it was beginning to seem as if she was screwed if she got married and she was some sort of failure if she didn't. What was she to do? Should she walk away now? She must be losing her mind. He loved her and he was not the same as all those selfish guys to her. They had years and years of experience with misbehaving. Her man was still new to this game and Mr. Tell Me Anything had been raised in the heart of the country. It was a slower paced environment.

"Country men are good men, right? His pace is at zero right?" Sharon remembered him driving to the city in his grandmother's stolen station wagon. With her Mama gone, all she needed was him to pass the time away and humor her. Mr. Tell Me Anything had been a perfect candidate. She found it to be astonishing that he could rise above his life of unfortunate circumstances all the while with a smile as they laughed the days away until he made it big. She remembered visiting his home in the country and thinking "how in the hell is he so happy?" His life of poverty had given her a new perspective on hers. Just when she thought she had nothing left she had met someone who never had anything. So with the thought of having her, she figured he would be content.

"So, why am I questioning him now?"

She had been so far from the average chick from his hometown. She had her father's brains, her mother's beauty and her very own apple bottom ass. Yes, she had that *ass*! It made most men go crazy but Mr. Tell Me Anything was a slight bit different. He actually hated to see the print of her female goods, always complimenting Sharon when she was fully dressed in skirts or dresses that flared out. He loved to see her in clothing that did not reveal any of her curves, all natural with no makeup…..but not at his games. She loved feeling simply beautiful when he would stare as she got dressed and undressed.

"So, why in the hell are these heifers trying to convince me that he is knocking off this skinny bitch with extra teeth in her mouth, plastic soles underneath her shoes and zits covering her horse face? They are so crazy."

The weekend came and so did the family barbecue. The couple was trying to initiate some bonding and healing. To her surprise, it went very well. It was actually much more than she expected. Everyone was laughing and having a great time. It was as if all the drama was behind them now. His family seemed very pleased with her cuisine and even threw out several comments like "I didn't know you could cook." Mr. Tell Me Anything seemed so proud of her today. He sat back and soaked it all in as the sun began to set. They were finally falling in love with her too. They had surprisingly warmed up after six years and five million dollars! Maybe they could work this out.

"All they need now is six million dollars next time and I will take formal cooking classes." She gagged. "No wait, maybe he'll get ten million and I will become a personal chef. Anything to make him happy," she thought, as she let out a little screech. His dad caught it and cut his eyes at her as she gave him the *I don't really like you either grin.* "Give me a break here."

It was perfect still. They now had an understanding. Why didn't he really like her anyway? Well, for starters she was four years his son's senior. She happened to be the prettiest thing you'd ever want to see and don't forget that apple bottom ass that filled up those size ten jeans on the spot. Oh, please incorporate the naturally flat stomach after two children, adorned with her newly purchased diamond belly ring. There were also several rumors concerning all the "top guys" that she had dated before. Hardly any of them were true but she didn't care to offer any justification because it was her business to tell or not. And besides, it was none of his concern what she did with her life or her kitty cat. Being unmarried, it always baffled her as to how *married people* had so much time to be so nosey. "If you're in love, who has that kind of time?"

Maybe he was miserable. She really didn't know. She was convinced of one thing though; his dad knew she was rocking his young ass every night. His thoughts were all together accurate except he excluded the fact that she was being rocked as well. Mr. Tell Me Anything had mad skills in the bedroom. She had taught it all to him. She couldn't believe that the heifers thought he was practicing his skills on that lying female from the arena.

After everyone was fed and full, Mr. Tell Me Anything retired to his favorite lamb skin, leather recliner. Their son was propped up in his favorite chair, too.......Mr. Tell Me Anything's lap. He had his cell phone in hand and began to retrieve his messages. He was taunting himself back and forth asking why his machine was so full...... "What in the hell do these people be wanting?"

Then Sharon heard Miss Stacked's voice because their two year old grabbed it and pushed speakerphone on accident. His reaction time was off because the family was around and he was blindsided. Their son had been quite swifter than him. Before he knew it, his ass was on blast! He could see the stunned look on her face but, there was no time to shut it off.

"This is Miss Stacked. I guess you are going to do the *family thing* today, so call me when you get free."

"The family thing? What in the hell? How in the hell did she get your number? Can you hear.....How did she get your number?"

"Baby wait..... she was just asking about the...."

"It doesn't matter *what* she was asking, how did she get *your* number? Call that bitch back right now!"

"Baby, calm down, I ain't calling her back, you need to trust me."

"I'm so sick of this trust bullshit.....Fine; I'm going to go get me a drink."

At this point and time they had gained an audience of an amused two. That was enough for her to have a double shot. She had already had a double shot of the lies, she had already had a double shot of the fake smiles, and the next double would be on the house. With a hard drink in hand she precluded to a quiet place of solitude where she began to question his actions over and over again. Why wouldn't he call her back? Was everything they said true? Was he really screwing her every chance he got? If so, it must have been great sex because her face and those teeth were deal breakers to Sharon. She often heard that ugly girls did *any* and *every*thing. Should she really take this serious? The way it was given to her, he was driving straight to the spot, banging her skinny ass and throwing her a couple of dollars for gas, plus free game tickets here and there.

"That's okay, I've got my drink and next time he can get her cheap ass to make barbeque for his fake ass folks." She could hear his voice through the sheetrock that was separating them. He was calling her name as if nothing had ever happened. As she was trying to brush by and make her way upstairs he grabbed her ass. He wanted to make this go away instantly to appease his family, saving face with them. First drink in hand, second drink on him and she stormed upstairs.

"Keep your damn hands off of me! I don't know where they've been."

This time she'd gone too far. As she climbed the stairs he chased her like a terrible two year old. The entire family began to whisper as if they weren't within hearing distance.

A female's voice whispered, "I told you she be tripping."

Then someone asked, "Well, why did he give her that big ass ring then?"

"He need to beat her ass!" Others were saying "We knew this was bound to happen." And they all whispered and conspired as her heart melted. It was clearer than ever that their perfect life was turning into a perfect mess already.

Some thought of the catastrophe as funny. There was no one on her side. They had all destined them to fail, every one of them barbeque eating bitches. Sharon absorbed all the humiliation and thoughts of wasted cooking and cleaning.

She could feel him grab her arm saying, "Baby please, just listen to me."

Not caring that family was in hearing distance, "I'm sick of you and your bitches and all of your lies. I'm going to bed."

She was in pain. Her mind wavered as she climbed the final step "I might have expected a mixed girl with hair down to her behind or any female with an educational background equivalent to mine who drove a Benz or Bentley. But this broke, stacked teeth bitch has no place in our life. What in the world is he thinking? He definitely isn't thinking about me. He isn't thinking about our kids and he isn't thinking about our future. This is bad. This is really really bad. I thought professional sports was supposed to raise the bar of standards. He seems to be digressing, perhaps even losing his freaking mind. Maybe I should just get him some help. Is he on drugs now? He's only been a professional a couple of months and he is now screwing women that resemble drag queens. Damn, this new life with all *this* money is gonna be worse than I ever thought."

The brilliant glare from her engagement ring was not going to be able to blind her from this one. This crap was getting more raggedy by the day. Now she had ugly stacked teeth drag queens in their circle.

"Does he like boys now? I have got to find this man a church. He is losing his way too quickly. Hell, we just got here. Somebody needs to stop and talk some sense into him. Does it have to be me again? He makes my ass hurt."

After the family left he began his big spill over again. This time his begging had afforded her three karat diamond earrings that were to be purchased in the morning. It was to be three carats in each ear as a matter

110

of fact. She loved the jewelry store in the Marina. It was their favorite place to shop after he got caught in his enormous lies. It had been their second home for the past couple of months and her jewelry box was so loaded that she began to daydream about heisting things from herself for fun. After more empty promises and mad make up sex (yes that was one of the better benefits) she knew she would forgive him. He had a way of making her forget things in less than twenty-four hours.

As the late evening crept in, they both showered together. They said their goodnights and she was all ready for bed, being completely worn out. He decided to go down and join his folks for a final drink and to lock up. She could hear his voice and their ridiculous jokes followed by his irresistible laugh. As she reviewed their day and the questions surrounding Miss Stacked, she discovered that he had left his cell phone attached to his pants pocket on the floor near the clothes basket. JACKPOT!!!!!! She had known the code beforehand but she had to *have* the damn phone to get into it. Now was her chance. She was anxious and filled with fear. She couldn't breathe or think. "Please keep him laughing" she thought. Sharon took a deep breath and she typed it in ever so carefully not to set off the alarm. 1-9-1-1. Yes, she was in! One after the other they had left their messages. Her heart stopped beating the entire time. She had died over and over again as they had left their seductive messages. He had left his passion marks all over her naked body. As she looked down at the ones between her thighs she heard one call him by nickname. Some called him by his proper name and there were even others that called him by names she never ever heard before.

But there was one voice that stood out from the rest. Being raspy and direct she spoke, "Why don't you come and give me some of that dick today?"

She did not leave her name but she left several previous messages that indicated her. With a voice like that, there was no mistaking this chick.

Suddenly, Miss Stacked seemed real. Her fiancé had a 1-900 whore calling him. Her voice was so sleazy that it aroused the senses. It was a saved message......he didn't discard it.

For a moment she sat there and mimicked her over and over again. "Why don't you give me some of that dick today?" The seductive bitch was a genius! She mastered the art of talking a man with two kids and a drop dead gorgeous fiancé into transporting dick over to her on a daily basis........."mobile dick.....now that's a concept."

Sharon was pulverized. She had never talked to him in *that* way before. "She is one up on me. This whore is the ultimate sex machine. I am the silly supermom; she is exotic, erotic. She's a sexy being. Why did I have all these damn kids anyway? My new life is screwed now."

One woman's voice had shaken her to her core. Everything she had worked so diligently for had been destroyed with a 1-900 Whore. She could not comprehend it all at once. She really thought they were on track.

But, he had assisted the phone queen in ruining her life. She had mistaken him with his freaking life plan and his "you're going to have all my babies" bullshit. Was his "big happy family plan" just a ploy to confine her to the house while he's out living the *good* life bringing women dick on the daily? With all his 1-900 whores and several secret callers, he had been so convincing all this time. When his cell phone rang at 1:00 am on just last week he argued that the female on the other end had the wrong number. When questioned the week before about another call the female had been a friend of a friend that was playing a prank of some kind on him. He even persuaded her to call the friend, who readily answered detailed enough to detour her suspicions. Either he had been telling the truth or they had rehearsed for extended hours.

It seemed she was spending the majority of her time these days differentiating between his blatant lies and the transparent truth. Though she had not been employed for two years now, lie detecting had become her newfound career. She was not getting any better at it either. Each time the lies became more convincing. Though she vowed never to become a complacent "rich bitch", she had settled into that very position naturally by default.

As the deception escalated, so did her monthly allowance. Who had time to keep up with his women and schemes while shopping on Rodeo Drive and rocking newborn babies? His money was poisonous.

She then determined that being his mother was for his *mother*. Oh yeah, she had quit her job after the draft, so she needed something to do anyways. Everybody had quit after that. (But that's another story) Nevertheless Sharon would leave raising her grown ass son to *her* and his phone whores. She had her own blue eyed Jr. to rear and from what she had already experienced, she wasn't going to let him out of her sight. He needed her. Everyone was not this lucky. Her son was going to have a great relationship with his mom and God and learn to honor, love and appreciate all the women in his life.

Sharon felt undeserving of his destructive type of behavior. She gave him everything that a man could ask for. All she needed from him in return was his honesty and love. It was time for her to get it together for her son and let him get it together for himself. She wasn't going to hold his hand this time. Then he tipped in.

"Why are you on my phone?"

"No, why are these bitches on your phone? You're a liar, that's all you do is lie. Why even bother lying, just say hey baby I'm a whore and I don't want this. I just want to whore around with whomever I want......why don't you just leave?"

"That's not what I want." Holding his phone in one hand and crocodile tears in his eyes, "Baby, this right here is some bullshit. I was just trying to fit in. Baby this shit is hard. All the dudes be cheating and making fun of me because I'm young, got two kids and in love. They mess with me saying "dude you all in love and shit" I'm just trying to fit in. Even my folks be saying that shit...like I'm too young to get married and I need to sleep with more women and stuff like that but, I don't want *nobody* but you. Please, I hate it when you cry. I will give all this shit up today, just please don't leave me."

He was putting it all out there. She needed to stand by him in this moment of despair. He could see the error of his ways and he was crying out for her immediate help. She could not leave him at a time like this. He needed her. This boy was struggling. She would just work on being sexier. He had no one else to turn to. His family's only interest these days seemed like taking his money and seeing how many free tickets they could acquire for bragging rights. If she left now, she didn't fully love him. He would be on his own. He was her baby. Hell, she had had him since he was two days over sixteen years old, though he had lied about his age. But yes....... she was the one he had looked to in his times of trouble, forever.

"I can't desert my baby." Nope, she was not going to do it, not her. She could never live with herself and that type of guilt. He wouldn't make it without her.

She didn't allow her mind to cancel out her new claim to love unconditionally. She stamped the proclamation with her very heart. "Done deal….. Wonder what he is going to buy me tomorrow." Then she snatched him down onto their bed of security and ravished him once again *with no hands* until he fell fast asleep. "Lord please him to be *stronger*, I love him God. Amen."

CHAPTER 6
THE BIG DAY

It was the brightest morning of June Sharon had ever seen in her twenty-eight years of living. Her head ached from the apple martinis and her skin reeked of stale men's cologne from the raunchy stripper that professionally performed for her the night before. One of her cousins, Amanda, had gotten her money's worth. Though his dance and body were superb and she had been flipped upside down a time or two in the process, her mind kept gravitating back to the soon-to-be father-in-law's voice.

"She's going to get the same thing going out as she had coming in to this marriage." Mr. Tell Me Anything let her listen on speaker as he tried frantically to coax him into presenting the document.

Damn! Did he exclude the fact that two of his grandchildren were already born and his son was begging for number three? As she heard it ring over and over again, she continued with her steaming hot shower for over thirty full minutes. The water drops just as well should have been teardrops.

Sharon traveled to a peaceful moment in time where there was no pain. She was only fifteen years old then. She was an inspiring clarinet section leader with unlimited ability, the envy of all eighth graders wanting to enter the High School Band. She had nabbed the starting second base position on the High School Softball Team after only one tryout, only to be struck out once the entire season. Her life had been one full of blessings. She watched her father become extremely proud of her. She was super athletic, very driven and successful. He had always thought that she possessed his heart of strength and all the talent that God could possibly give a child. She had his total support with her Honor Society status and her perfect smile. Now here she stood with scented body wash covering her wounds like bandages because of all their drama. No one wanted this for them.

Just two days prior to her early summer wedding day her Father-in-law decides that a prenuptial agreement was necessary. She guessed he was running out of time. So, after much counsel was given by her dad's attorney, the great Tim Hodges, Sharon signed the ridiculous document. Little did his father know, she and her fiancé had discovered that you must give a potential spouse at least seven days to overlook a document of that magnitude in the State of California. According to the state laws that year, the money grubbers were all in for the shock of their lives if their marriage turned south. The agreement was totally invalid. She could see his dad now, sitting with the calculator and his generic attorney, like the one who drew it up, while she walked in to crack their faces. But for now, she decided to let him believe what he wanted to believe. Ronald Smart was not so smart after all......

"Where did they get his license anyway........in the crackerjack box?"

"It's our own comedy show now starring the Poor Thing, Mr. Tell Me Anything, having to inform Mr. I Don't Know a Damn Thing that he placed his son's fate in the hands of Mr. I Got Paid For Nothing…..while my wife and I knew everything." Her stomach hurt from the laughing pains.

"It's not my fault…….. God, thank you for my Daddy, full of wisdom and all equipped with important friends that are *real* lawyers." Sharon began to chuckle thinking how she would spring the truth on his father who had reached a false level of confidence, believing he had totally secured his son's fortune. Maybe she would never have to mention it and they would just both go to their graves knowing he's a ridiculous, greedy, selfish interfering soul.

Mr. Tell Me Anything was not in agreement with the pre-nuptial at all. In fact, he tried to convince his father that it was unnecessary so that Sharon would somehow let it go. He explained all the way; he was very unhappy about putting it all on her at the last second and felt about strongly wanting her to be alright regardless of how it turned out. His father didn't hear a word of it though. He was convinced Sharon would run away with everything that *he* wanted. Besides that…..he was not going to rest until she knew that she was not number one. "Sorry Papa." The ink is dry now and we've all made our stance.

"Oh crap! "Sharon realized she had only twenty minutes to get to her wedding at the country club where she was scheduled to wed at noon. It was a thirty minute drive but she took her sweet little time because she was scared half to death. "Well, they can just all wait. "

Sharon entered the enormous building on the west side. She was immediately joined by two ecstatic bride's maids who were astonished to see that her hair was a complete mess. Her swollen eyes were more of a mess and this wedding with greedy family members and crackerjack lawyers was the biggest mess of it all. She sat in the hot seat as her frizzy hair and makeup were being perfected and then she panicked and completely froze.

"Let me look out, I need to see him."

"You can't because the guests will see you and we are already running behind," from the maid of honor. "It's bad luck. Be still before she sticks you in the eye." The mascara was going on thicker than ever.

"I don't care because I need to see his face now."

"Okay just one peep!"

As she squinted through the solid wood double doors she could see that he looked very presumptuous at the end of the aisle. He was beaming with joy like a kid at Christmas time. Her man was dressed to kill in his custom tuxedo that she selected and ordered. It was off-white and the vest had a hint of silver and gold variations running through it like little veins, flawless. It was the only thing that he allowed her to do. He planned everything else himself. He was so suave standing there.

"Damn he is everything to me."

She forgot about the signed invalid document. She forgot about the family and friends who were only concerned with having it signed. She forgot about his parents all dressed in black for a summer wedding.

"If they burn up today they might feel right at home. I'm going to be his wife in a matter of moments." (Deep Breath) "Okay, I'm okay y'all. Do you guys think I need to wear this one or that one?"

They all giggled and agreed that it didn't matter what lingerie she chose to wear because with their history he wasn't going to waste any time removing it. He had been a "sure thing" right from the start, which didn't actually begin until he was four months shy of his eighteenth birthday. Her family would joke about how she was robbing the cradle with their apparent age difference. Nobody wanted her to go to jail. But, even the best of debaters couldn't convince her that he was not the one.

She loved this man at first sight. But with all her majestic feelings present, Sharon still felt a bit of anger and sadness this day grounded in the obvious fact that despite her efforts to be a survivor and good wife, her Mama would miss the occasion. She herself was divorced by her dad and killed by her cancer. She had loved her husband severely as Sharon did her husband-to-be. She had three children, eighteen months a part, boy then girl then boy again. Sharon was on the same roll. But today she would be missing on the most important day of a girl's life.

"She just died way too soon," she thought. "She will never meet my children or this man I am about to marry. She should definitely be here today." Sharon held back the tears.

"Is my hair alright.....? No tell me the truth. Did you remember the plane tickets? What about the other limo? I wonder if the food is going to be good. Is anybody else starving besides me? Did she they make it here with the cake? It wasn't here earlier. They sent a voicemail." She was getting more nervous as the four hundred guests continued to pile in.

"Just calm down, we good up in here. Everything is in place. The cake is beautiful." The matron of honor finally spoke up.

"We're good?"

"Yes, you're good, you guys are in love, forget about everybody else and focus on him and the wonderful life you guys are going to have together."

"So good that nothing is going to keep us apart either, honey, let's do this."

The music began and they all left her alone one by one. They exited on cue drifting down the long staircase decorated with all white roses toward the huge arch with their positions beside it. They all looked totally exquisite. She had selected bronze laced dresses with gold undertones and they were each wearing golden accessories. Everyone was equipped with shimmery body gleamers to hold in extra curves and sleek satin shoes covered their elegant feet. It was a sight to see! All of her friends and family had lost up to twenty pounds each. Nothing was going to ruin her day or her $10,000 photo shoot. She had told the heavier ones that they were going to be a fourteen or they were going to watch it from the audience. Obviously, she had made herself very clear.

Hers was the local wedding of the century with an expected guest list of over four hundred plus ninety-five additional people. It was a combination of fake family members, jealous ex-girlfriends, one night stand victims, other prominent Memphians and ball players, her dad's co-workers and half the population from the country, both known and unknown. In addition, there were some that loved their union and teenage girls with grand delusions of meeting their princes and becoming their brides. They were all there. She had never attended a wedding where all the guests arrived on time. This was a first. There was much speculation as to what she would be wearing and if she'd wear her *real* hair on today. Of course not, a girl needed at least two tracks to hold the style together for a day such as this one. Other speculation was grounded in the fact that some family members had wished her limo was crushed by an eighteen wheeler but God saw to it that she arrived safely even with her frozen feet and grieving heart. Today was the big day! As the last bride's maid exited, her maid of honor, winked at her with glassy eyes filled with joy and anticipation.

"You straight?"

"Girl, what do you think?"

The door closed behind her and she was all alone with the exception of one very young cousin to announce her entrance. She had rehearsed her part over and over again. "The bride is coming, the bride is coming." That's what she was instructed to do. Her mind wandered to her proposal in the limousine then it made its way to their first kiss. Her brain was so clustered with glimpses of his smile and the sweet sensation that overtook her body when he touched her. She could smell the distinct aroma of his warm breath as it breathed on her every night for the past six and a half years. She could not train these thoughts to stop. She thought of the first time he went inside of her and how intense it had been after waiting sixteen months and how he held back his ejaculation for more than twenty minutes at the age of seventeen. He looked down at her and said "I love you and was it okay." To this very day she had made him believe it was alright but she knew that night that she would never let another man touch her in that way. He was a giving lover, full of passion and desire. He had graduated from a little shy to being very verbal in their love making.

One of the hardest things about being captured by her younger man was the fact that he was still under the influence of his parents and his juvenile friends. But somehow he had broken out of the mold and been a generous man with a huge heart and an oversized partner to share with her at night. Sharon had waited so patiently for him touch her life in that way.

Their first night together was so special. She thought of how she rewarded him for all his troubles of standing in the drenches with her after the loss of her Mama. They took it slow from the beginning but the anticipation was more than they could overcome....so they gave in to their lust. She thought originally to allow him to finish school first but they had spent way too much time alone. It was the inevitable. It was explosive to say the least. It was like a fairy tale...the best sex she'd ever had. He laid beside her that night with her head nestled into the folds of his arms. She wanted to stay there forever. He told her over and over again that she had been worth waiting for. She wondered how much more different it would be tonight as his wife. She wondered what it would feel like to sleep with her husband, to have him ravage her naked body. She didn't really see how it could get any better than it already was. Their sex was the bomb!

Sex left her mind and her fears resurfaced. "Does he automatically realize this is *it* or will we face the same issues?" Sharon was tormented by the previous lies but she was determined not to let them stop her from making it down that aisle. Besides she was too damn beautiful in her dress.

"I'm ready!" Besides, her daddy would kill her for wasting all his money. He had wanted to pay at least a large portion of the fees.

Sharon wanted to marry him. She had been waiting for him for almost seven years. Today was going to be the best day of the rest of her life. "You only get out of life what you invest in it. "

She detached her spirit from all the confusion of the cell phone drama and all the things that didn't add up. All her worries and unfortunate circumstances would be summed up today at the end of that aisle. Today she would finally rest from the madness of deception. He would shut the mouths of all the spectators and fake family members. Maybe one day they would realize that this was a true love and they had lost the battle in spite of their determinations. It was only *her* that had won the prize. He would be *her man* at last! "I am going to be Mrs. Tell Me Anything in less than fifteen minutes."

"It's time." Her daddy whispered as he held out his strong arm. The two grown men she loved the most in the world were in the same building wearing the same color with the same look on their faces. One was to give her away and the other waiting impatiently for him to do so. They were very close to each other. Sometimes he talked to her dad more than her. She didn't mind though because he needed a male connection. They were always in agreement with one another about her being spoiled. And today they both agreed on this one important thing, to marry him would be more cost efficient for her dad.

She watched the sun illuminate through the widening windows of the ball room. The chairs were neatly seated in the passageway and filled with all their friends, family and guests. She was about to transition from baby mother to bride in a matter of moments. There would be no better time like the present to run as fast as she could in the other direction. The aisle was free and clear now. She could reach the back exit door in less than thirty seconds.

"Okay, breathe girl." She kept promising herself that she was doing the right thing and that things would get better as they both got more mature. She would maintain the household and put in more time with him and the children. There was hard work involved in holding things so valuable together. With their love for each other, they could do this. They both *want* to do this. She placed her brain on autopilot for a moment.

"Do you take this man..................."

"I Do."

It was over. She could breathe and smile now or did she smile first and then breathe? Maybe she should just scream because everyone has this conquered look on their faces. She didn't know what to do. So she did what she had done best all these years. She reached right out and threw her slender arms around the elevated neck of the man of her dreams. They took their first dance as husband and wife.

Their overall experience had taught her one concrete thing, she knew how to love a man and she had chosen who that man was going to be. It didn't matter what was being said, she loved him. It didn't matter who he screwed in the past, she loved him. It didn't matter that his family didn't understand her, she loved him. It didn't matter what anyone in the whole wide world thought, she loved him. And today he made her Mrs. Tell Me Anything with everyone as their witnesses. He loved her. There was no stopping them now. This would be the marriage of every girl's dream. They would stop and stare and stand in awe of this amazing true love. She had convinced herself of this with his help and their romantic ceremony. She could no longer hear his previous words. The only two words echoing in her mind today were…..……."I do."

Yes, this would be the beginning of their new life together as husband and wife. "God, thank you for bringing us this far. I love him, Amen."

CHAPTER 7
BLISS

Sharon was still in her pajamas; at least that's what she called his oversized T-shirt and her barely there G-string panties. It had been a very long night due to the game going into double overtime. He still had to work the next day, so she was catching up on her rest as usual when he was away. The *Young and the Restless* was sensational from her bed, it was her favorite show to watch always starting around the time she woke up. She had no plans to set foot out of the bed until he returned today. When the commercials started, she could hear the nanny stroll the upper level hallway while humming a familiar song to new her baby. "She must be almost asleep," Sharon thought.

Janet Taylor had been hired by Sharon after meeting her in a local department store and finding her to be one of the most pleasant people she had ever met. Though she barely knew her, the young mother had prayed about the safety of her newborn because she had just lost a daughter to sudden infant death syndrome the year before. She had been with their family three whole years now, stealing her away from her own. With the new employee at her side, Sharon had made her way back to becoming secure again. But this child would be her last. Though she personally disapproved of babies being rocked to sleep...she had allowed it under the circumstances. This lady was wonderful with kids....like a dream come true. Besides, Sharon loved her gray hair and her Sunday Schooled ways. She was a frequent churchgoing woman with kids and grandkids of her own, this was always a plus. It was like a free trial to watch her with them before the couple decided to make her permanent. They jumped at the opportunity.

Sharon's guess was that Janet had believed that she was still asleep. Because despite her parental commandments, she was spoiling the newborn to no end. She knew there was no harm intended. Janet simply couldn't help herself. The baby loved this lady and this lady thought she belonged to her.

As Sharon listened mindfully, she couldn't seem to rest. All she could think of was the fact that her husband was getting a whole weekend and an entire day off. She wondered what they would do with the kids. They all needed a break and some quality time together.

Their new life after marriage was full of love and various surprises. He was a very spontaneous man. This made loving him *fun*. On his silly days, he would bust through the front doors saying, "honey I'm home," trying to scare her. She was always a *huge* scaredy cat. She would scream hysterically as he fell into the floor laughing. Sometimes she was so afraid and mad that she would even tackle him. Then after about ten minutes he would laugh even harder remarking, "Girl, you ain't stronger than me."

They had all sorts of games that they played with one another. When she would leave their bed after midnight sex, to grab a drink at his request, he would jump out of the bed, hide around the corner of the kitchen, lay flat on the floor like a marine and grab her ankles in the darkness. This one made her furious! He had loved to see her mad. Call it crazy, but he was so silly like that.

"Hey, honey I'm home. Where is everybody?"

This time Sharon jumped out of the bed, hid in his closet and waited. She was gonna show him how to scare somebody.

"Baby, where are y'all?"

He was way too lazy to hit the staircase and just knew that she had dared to climb them herself, so he started his search on the first floor. She could hear him opening and closing door after door. He even checked the garage. She began laughing her butt off.

Then she heard him talking to himself saying, "Where is her ass at? I'm hungry."

This made her laugh even harder because she wasn't about to cook him anything. He had let the chef off for today. Someone should have suggested that he think this thing through. Then, she heard him pick up his cell phone. He called her cell at least three times but it was dead. "Thank God. "

He had given up and started walking towards his closet just when she reached out and grabbed his neck after he passed her. He jumped up and did a karate stance in midair on his way down. She gagged for thirty minutes until he started chasing her all the way outside into the cove while she yelled, "somebody, call the police," but there was no one around, the coast was clear. It then occurred to her, she wasn't going to be able to leave the room tonight because he was most definitely going to pay her back.

When all the madness ceased he called Janet down to make a family announcement. "Look you and my wife need to pack the kids' stuff because we leave for the Bahamas in three hours."

"Why did you wait till the last minute to tell us?"

"Because I was too busy chasing her crazy ass down the street. But don't worry, that ass is mine when she least expects it."

"Baby please, I'm sorry."

"Naw, I don't wanna hear it. I'm gonna get that ass back when you least expect it."

Damn! She was horrified and instantly horny. He said that like he meant it. She could see it in his little evil eye. She laughed all the way to the kid's dresser drawers. Beaming with joy, she placed their little shirts, pants and socks into their Eddie Bauer luggage that she had just purchased for them. She didn't realize they would use it this soon but it made a small amount of her guilt settle.

She had paid way too much for those six pieces. She needed all of them in case someone else would tag along.

"Okay, now the nanny could use one too." She laughed again. "Today is such an awesome day so far."

After they were done she had to call the travel agent to push back the flights for two more hours. At this point she didn't have anything done for herself and her daughter's hair was still in poor condition. She admitted to herself that her daughter needed to stay home with her head looking that way because she did not want to tackle it. She tried to see what would become of the tight curls as she proceeded with caution, she was tender headed. She never really understood why the people with the nappiest heads had the nerve to holler "ouch." She felt it necessary they had all the combs and brushes they could possibly get in there. It suddenly dawned on her that she didn't have sandals. "Who goes to the hottest place they know without a decent pair of sandals? My God, she is going to fit right in over there with an afro and bare feet! This isn't working. I need more time. "

They were almost off to a weekend getaway just like that; Sharon was completely mesmerized by it. It was so adventurous of him. He had a way of whisking her away like that all the time. He had been that way from the very second day after they met. She had been attending a game, out of respect for her father, and it was pouring down raining afterwards. She was standing right in the door of the gym with newly pressed hair and her fluffy toy poodle in hand. She was terrified at the thought of getting either of their heads completely soaked. While holding them and scanning the parking lot for her car, Mr. Tell Me Anything snatches her keys right out of her hand and starts running, calling back to her, "which one?" As she cried out, "that one" he hit the alarm and jumped inside. He drove as close as he could to the gym door's entrance but there was a sidewalk and a large concrete area separating the parking lot from the door. In order to avoid her getting a *drop* of water on her, he hops the curb and pulls right up to the door. She could remember the security officer look right at her and smile saying, "Now that's curb side service." As everyone watched, he hopped out, covered her head with his uniform shirt and said "get inside." He was her hero, fearless. And now, he was even more fearless trying to pull together four children at the last minute to travel the friendly blue skies.

"It's okay. I'm going to make this work, *no* sandals and all."

After defeating her head, Sharon set out to the local bank. She liked to travel with decent amounts of cash. She also stopped by and got snacks for the kids for their plane ride. She selected chips, cookies, crackers, peanuts and sunflower seeds. The last two things on her list were her favorite gum and his favorite magazine," got it!" Now everyone would have what they needed. As for herself, she also needed to pull her hair back into a ponytail and let her beauty shine through….so she also grabbed some twister beads. She made it back to the house as they were loading up the bags.

As she watched the luggage being shoved into the family van, she reflected back to the birth of their twins. They now had plenty of additions. She could remember the news of carrying the twins after originally going to be checked out for potential pregnancy problems. Her thinking was that there was a problem with all the spotting. She had sent up several prayers before her appointment because she felt too much lower pressure in her stomach. The Dr. took his machine, looked inside and said, "Oh, I see the problem here. Your placenta is covering your cervical area." It sounded really scary as he continued. "But the babies are fine."

"Babies!!! "

"Yes, see there is *Baby A* and there is *Baby B*, all in-tact. They are right there in the same sack…see? You will be fine, just put your feet up for a couple of days."

"Who told him that? How did he think that having two babies at a time was going to make me be okay? What about stretch marks and dirty diapers? What am I going to do?" Sharon had no idea.

Nonetheless Mr. Tell Me Anything's reaction was quite different. She had never seen a man that excited about a pregnancy. He was shouting so loud that the gas attendant came outside to watch him. Can you imagine a local celebrity screaming his head off in a public parking lot standing by a gas pump? "I'm having twins!!!"

"Now I'm standing here thinking how can he get all those heavy bags and extra suitcases in that van? Find that out and that would make me shout. I need all that stuff."

"Where have you been?"

She pulls his magazine out and says, *"Getting us ready for our trip."*

He looks at the book, laughs, and says, "I don't need that, all I need is them little bikinis you gonna be squeezing that *entire* ass into until you get the kids to sleep."

She switched away to the door. She was throwing it until he started his singing a song out loud that made her pause at the front door and pretend to be a stripper. She was dropping it like it was hot over and over, then the nanny returned with another bag.

"See...... you almost got caught," he said.

Then they both busted out laughing while she had that perplexed look on her face. "Y'all are crazy."

"Honey if you only knew that you were living with a fool and his personal...stripper...... we are great together." Sharon was glad that Janet missed her performance. She was much too sweet to behold such things coming from the young mother.

The family made it to the airport in a snap. As they boarded the plane, Sharon imagined the love they would make over the course of their stay. She thought of the sexy walks on the beach at night and the skinny dipping. Because the children were tagging along, she had to organize her thoughts of the activities they would encounter. "Oh my God, they simply love that day camp at the resort." On their last vacation to the Bahamas her daughter had a tantrum when they picked her up fifteen minutes earlier than the other day campers. She was so upset about missing the end of the camp song. She had wanted to stay forever. And Sharon had thought the very same thought on her last day at the hotel casino because she had had a lucky streak. The couple had even considered retiring over there. They could just envision the sand and half nakedness for eternity. It was really odd to Sharon that he would agree on such a plan because Mr. Tell Me Anything hated the blazing sun. But he sought to please her and make her dreams a reality as she had done his so many times in the past.....Her Love.

The plane landed after the smoothest ride they'd flown in months. The kids practically slept the entire way. It was so peaceful to look into their faces not knowing what the rest of the day would hold for them. As they slept, the parents played with each other's feet the whole way. It was very arousing, so much so that they both did a b-line to the bathroom. They had been in the mile high club ever since they had their first flight together. By the time they got to their destination, sex was the last thing on their minds. They wanted to see the kids "kick it." As soon as the bell hop, took their bags and they checked in, they headed straight to the swimming pools! On Paradise Island, there were so many sights to see but today, they only saw the pool. The nanny and the kids were enjoying themselves. The frozen drinks we were served up, it was perfect. He gazed intently over at her and said, "Baby, I wish we could stay here forever."

She responded, "Yeah, me too."

He didn't know how much she really meant it. There were no friends there, no real groupies there, always one lurking though. There was no family there. It was only them and their children together in Bliss.

"What a gorgeous family," another father exclaimed from the poolside.

"Thank you," Mr. Tell Me Anything agreed.

They heard that same statement just about everywhere they had gone. They had spent hours and hours and years and years debating about how they *got* so gorgeous. She thought it was her cheekbones and her complexion. He thought it was his teeth and his smooth dark skin. They went on and on with the debate always ending in, "so, you like it," on both sides. All and all he had loved her appearance and she, his! They *were* such a gorgeous family! God had been so good to them both. The sun was hot, life was good, their love was strong and their growing family was picture perfect.

CHAPTER 8
MISS HONEY BLONDE

Sharon decided it was her time to lie to her husband for a change. He had been harassing her for well over an hour. Mr. Tell Me Anything delivered his third degree about her simply wanting fried chicken nuggets, all the while proclaiming she was only four weeks into her new diet. He could not comprehend what in the world was taking her so long to travel from their subdivision to the neighborhood Wendy's which was less than a mile away? Even a skilled bike rider should have made that condensed journey in a more adequate amount of time. But she lied.

She yearned so desperately for a number one combo from Krystal's and judging from his exact words, he was just leaving the local college basketball game. She only had a forty minute time window and she was determined to use it wisely. It had become so obvious to her right from the beginning that this crash diet thing was not going to work out. Being a mother of several small children, she was constantly encamped around a huge assortment various crackers, cookies, juice boxes and the inevitable, Mickie D's. For breakfast, the children always lusted for dripping buttery pancakes with pounds of syrup, followed by gallons of orange juice and at least three fried eggs each scrambled with American cheese. Her kitchen was like a heart attack waiting to happen. The pantry was so loaded that she kept the door secured at all times. It was saturated with everything you could imagine from animal crackers to at least five boxes of sugar coated breakfast cereals, all supersized. Their ceilings were twelve feet tall so your hungry eyes could start at the bottom shelf and become a victim of obesity by the time they reached the top. It was no hope for Sharon and her extra pounds in her home. So she committed to breaking free from the hunger pains of her own place and take the show on the road. "Krystal's here I come! "

She had it all figured out. She would chug them down and brush her perfect white teeth to minimize the distinctive smell. This would be the first night that she'd love to see that posse of his.

"So if they show, I would happily grant him the opportunity to babysit them while I gain a pound or two back."

The intruders normally proceeded straight to the third floor when they came to visit *each and every day*. "How could they even be comfortable being around every day? Don't you want to lounge on your own couch? Don't you want to take a dump in your own toilet? Don't you want to access your own refrigerator and guzzle down your own kid's Capri Sun juice boxes instead of mine? (But that's another story) I guess you can only do what you're allowed to do, so tonight I will authorize them and I'll keep my bedroom door fastened shut. I will let them focus on their silly video games and boyish activities. Then I can center *my* thoughts around losing the weight eventually."

"I am going to *eventually* do this....just in my own time," she thought. Besides, an extra 1500 calories wasn't going to kill anyone. If only she could cease to having kids. Nonetheless, she was now brave enough to venture out and grab her Krystal's. And thinking ahead, she did slide by Wendy's to cover her tracks. Now, if discovered, she would actually be free from being called a "real liar." She would simply inform Mr. Tell Me Anything (new father) of her true whereabouts with a brief justification of her starvation state and her need to eat more than three times a day.

"Hell, I am still breastfeeding. Does anyone else consider this?"

She was always breastfeeding. And this bird food diet was wearing her brain down. She needed something greasy today! Maybe she could say she was bringing the baby back some Krystal's too. He was a whopping five months old now and he was just starting his solid foods.

"Whoever said Krystal's wasn't healthy for us?"

Yes, she would say it was for the both of them. So it was up to her and her baby and their lack of nourishment to succeed. She took her chances and there was no way around it. She had to have what she needed when she needed it.

As she raced down the strip, she whipped passed his customized truck. "Where is he going?"

145

He was nowhere in the vicinity that he had just claimed to be. He had just hung up the telephone........ He lied. Where in the world was he going and why in the world was he harassing her about chicken nuggets? There were red flags flying everywhere.

"I knew something was strange...... I didn't deserve that kind of treatment. All that.......for wanting some chicken nuggets? Besides, he needs to lose fifteen pounds himself according to his trainer and the decline of his jumping ability. So what is this all about?"

It suddenly dawned on her that he was up to no good. The chicken nuggets had been a diversion the entire time. No individual in their right mind was that damn angry about a little cheating on a brand new diet. This was not adding up at all.

"I am so confused right now. Why would he....."Then she spotted her....... Miss Honey Blonde.

From the main street, Sharon had to pass his posse's townhouse in order to make it to the burger joint. She spotted her vehicle in the moonlight, parked in the middle of his friend's driveway. She had positioned it with authority as if the driveway somehow belonged to her, taking over half of it up with her hideous ride.

"Who drives a trap like that at her age? Surely the men receiving services from her could attempt to pitch in on something a little more accommodating. Is she a free whore? Those are the worst kind. They are the type that give it up *for free* and for the mere excitement of making a man crazy about them. If she isn't free, I know she's bold because I wouldn't park that piece of crap anywhere. "

Sharon's previous investigation had revealed that the beat up automobile definitely belonged to her and to make matters worse, she was still sitting inside of it as Sharon crept by. With her interior lights on, she caught a glimpse of her fluffing her Honey Blonde curls while anticipating her husband's arrival. She flicked off her headlights and hid in the cut thinking of all the rumors she had heard. Then she watched as he made a complete circle around the block before deciding that he would be dropped off in front of the house. She couldn't *actually see* the house from where she was parked now, but she knew it was about to go down. They all knew too.

"Am I some little pawn in some sick game of his played by him and the posse? Is he just that juvenile after all these years of marriage? I can't believe all of these bastards know about her and not a single one of them came forward to warn me. These same people eat at my dinner table all the damn time. They can't find the time in between free tickets, free chicken, free clothes and pocket change to inform me that my life is not my life? They may as well have helped him plan my funeral. Whatever happened to honesty and respect?"

The truck had personalized tags so obviously it couldn't be left at some scene. So after providing taxi service to Mr. Tell Me Anything, the black Escalade vanished into the night. He was brilliant, he thought...... But not brilliant enough!

God allowed this to happen because Sharon normally didn't give in to food temptation. Shopping was always her biggest weakness. On this particular night and this particular time, the stage was set for the showdown, throw down or time for the percolator as they called it in the early 90s. It was time for *something* since Miss Honey Blonde was repeatedly so "damn fat" in all his convincing lies. Forget about perfect figures, please believe, this chick was at least a size fourteen. All of her previous suspicions had been confirmed. She had been "fat this, and fat that" from the mouth of Mr. Tell Me Anything. Somebody was lying.

"So you're doing what with a fat bitch after being dropped off by your homies in a vacant house? How come all of y'all couldn't be up in there? Why do you and Miss Oversized need to be alone? "Her questions would soon be answered after crawling through a rear window, which was always left open. They were too trifling to keep up with keys. BULLSEYE, she was in! Sharon wasn't too familiar with the surroundings so she tripped over a crate in a pitch black room. As she searched the vicinity she didn't find any bedrooms on the lower level of the site.

"So he got that fat bitch upstairs?" As she quietly climbed the staircase, her heart rushed into her Gucci stiletto boots. She thought back to the days of their youth when it was just them. He had nothing but her and she had nothing but her broken heart and him to readily mend it. They had completed each other. His, was a story of strength and how he rose above the chains of poverty, abuse and neglect to become a good man. Hers was a story of survival and how she did not let the face of death and disappointments steal her from this world. She had more living to do, with a sense of purpose. They had faced the worst or so they thought and there was nothing or no one that could sever what wisdom and experience had given them both, each other.

Yet, there she stood midway up the stairwell. "Here I am in a smelly trap with him and this fat bitch!" She could hear loud screams of passion and hard breathing. She was hoping not to see what was becoming more evident by the second.

He was startled as he heard her footsteps grow closer and closer. "Who is that?" Then he peeped out, penis in hand with his slender body, completely naked, wearing only a condom.

"Oh my God!" He previously said he wouldn't sleep with her using someone else's penis. Well, she gave him *instant* credit because he *was* wearing the condom but the penis still belonged to him. He probably wished that he had borrowed someone else's penis *this* night for real.

"Okay now, tell me *another* lie. Lie about the fat bitch now!"

She was still hungry even though her appetite had changed from hunger pains in her stomach to hunger pains in her brain. She needed answers now! The sight of him and that damn condom was more than overwhelming.

"My God, he is my husband. I am his wife. This is our life. I would never ever let another man touch me, let alone see me naked. Oh my God!" Sharon had a little talk with Jesus.

"Now ....tell me another damn lie. Don't look at me like you're scared because baby violence is *your thing* remember? I'mma let you have your fat bitch, too."

After hurling several insults, she slapped the hell out of his ass. She swung so hard as she noticed the most important part of her life laying there isolated on the filthy floor, his wedding band. He had removed it before the opening ceremonies began. Maybe this was his cheater's ritual. He had placed their life on the ground.

She began screaming obscenities again at him until she realized that Miss Honey Blonde was nowhere in sight. She had hid in the adjoining bathroom. She had to kick the door in because she would not release it. She was in full commando mode at this point and there she was still in her black granny panties. Sharon hauled her from the bathroom by her hair and berated her with all sorts of vulgar names, things that she had never spoken before…….. Things only he had taught her. As she went at her with several excruciating blows to the head, it became such an awful event. "Mike Tyson…who?" Imagine the humiliating experience for a mother on her way to steal a Krystal moment. All she could think back to was having to avoid his fifty questions. They had come from his jealous ass, her so-called "soul mate." Her adrenaline ran so high but her heart ran extra low. "What a bunch of bull."

First, she had climbed through the window. Then she had climbed to the top of the stairs. That was too much energy. Their trifling asses didn't even keep the house secure. But she conceived that no one had time for home security when trafficking sluts in and out the jump off spot.

"They have slut trafficking right here in Memphis. You don't even have to go out of the country anymore. Yeah, I said it, got to call it like I see it. Who else is going to let a well-known celebrity screw them in a house (townhouse) that reeks of two week old trash and demolished beer bottles?" To add to the gruesome scene there was only a twin bug infested mattress on the floor in the room and a rusted file cabinet with missing doors. She found them there with no sheets, urine stains covering the filthy thing, and a whole floor filled with old condom wrappers and his ring. She was cheap and now began to seem somewhat desperate as Sharon began to critique her.

Wearing a size fourteen, Sharon just couldn't get past it. She was unable to wrap her mind around the double digits and his badgering her about her new diet in a size twelve. He hated heavy women and especially those with flat asses. There was obviously no comparison but yet and still Miss Honey Blonde was virtually naked in the jump off spot with her "Mr. Tell Me Anything." She had never caught him with another woman like that before. He would *always lie* his way out of every single thing. He would *always lie* himself out of every situation. He would *always lie* himself out of wrongful conversations. They would mostly argue over stupid phone calls and two hour time windows. They had never faced a *real live* situation like this one before. Her feelings wavered somewhere between furious and devastated. She just wanted to die on the spot. Underneath it all and to her surprise she still mustered up a slight giggle thinking of her flat ass and those damn granny panties. Even at that "time of the month" Sharon had worn thongs and tampons. Pads and panties were a no-no for her.

"Who screws a woman in granny panties? What kind of mess is that?" For a moment they both became desperate, small and beneath her. "I'm going to have his ass tested tomorrow," she thought.

He looked up at her with that pitiful ass look talking about "Baby, please."

152

She couldn't even stand the sound of his voice. His nasty trifling ass was standing there looking so stupid. It never dawned on him that he was still wearing that damn condom. In all the years that she had known him they never used condoms. He told her that he couldn't feel anything with them on.

"So, why ruin your marriage when you can't feel anything?" Then she smacked his ass again. With keys in her hand it had left a mark on his face....perfect! It was a sight to see. His face was all adorned in bright red blood and hers in black because of the smudged mascara and tears. They were even now. She was done.

"You bastard. You lying ass bastard."

She raced to her Lexus SUV infuriated. Hot on her trail was Mr. Tell Me Anything. Considering the circumstances surrounding this event, there was nothing he could tell her this night. He dove on the hood of her truck. She had to call on God this time because she kept thinking she should slam into reverse and let this compulsive liar go flying onto the pavement but she couldn't think it through. And they had too many spectators now. Besides....she could hurt him by leaving his ass. This alone would kill him.

In all the chaos, the posse had pulled back up to take him home. She wondered what they thought of her now. She had walked through her home daily in a stride that belonged to a queen. She had been bossy and rude on many occasions, a "rich bitch." Now here she was at a trap, bawling because her husband just bedded a fat slut on a pissed out mattress.

He was standing in the driveway begging and pleading. The begging part may have redeemed his ass in the past, but not tonight. She was still in the house recovering and hiding. Sharon wasn't quite sure of whose voice it was, but one of his crew members asked her; (with the window rolled down) "Are you okay?" So, she rushed over to the truck and then she slapped his ass, too. She had whipped everything in that mutha. Then she exclaimed to the driver "and don't bring your broke ass back to my house either...... User."

He was so pathetic and pitiful with all his fake tears. Sharon felt nothing as she began to yell "get off my car, let me go."

He responded, "Please let me talk to you, I don't want you to drive like this. If you are going to leave me, take me now."

She answered, "When you get done with this fat prostitute, your stuff will be outside. *Take yourself* to hell!"

"So, where are you going?"

"To Krystal's, all I wanted was ...."

The tears had begun to flood in. She cried a river in just a matter of seconds. She had placed a phone call to her girlfriend, Stephanie Parks, when she discovered his tags. She was the only one who would understand. She had been there for her through all of her insecurities. She was slightly older and managed to marry a male whore of her own. Most of their unfortunate experiences blended pretty well together. She always kept Sharon grounded and aware. She was smart and alert. Often she reminded her of her mom with her kindred spirit. Sharon could trust her. Patiently she waited in the cove nearby to talk some type of sense into her. When she came back to her senses she could hear the concern in her meek voice.

She began to humbly speak, "Stay calm, and think about the kids. After this he doesn't have a choice but to do right since all his lies have caught up to him. This can be a good thing for you guys. Try to look at it that way."

This all sounded good when she knew that she wasn't going to leave. "Yes, I'm living in a mansion, I have three nannies, I have two maids, a full time chef who happens to nice on the eyes and the man makes a mean omelet. I have two drivers and a gardener plus a pool man. I don't have to cook, clean, drive, fold clothes or anything. So, I'm going where? Yes to take a bubble bath of course and to call my masseuse who always has inspirational things to say. Besides that is the only time I have with Jesus these days." Sharon was way too busy for church with her traveling and enormous amount of responsibility surrounding celebrity wifehood and multiple children, motherhood. "I'm not going *no damn where*! He needs to take his ass on somewhere. I'm not leaving *my* house and *my* life, I will make *him* leave. I don't need him and his lies. I can handle this *by myself*. Me and my kids will be fine. Half of six million a year sounds great to me. Screw him! You nasty bastard! You liar!"

She could hear her mother's voice in the back of her brain and that was enough for now. Knowing she died over ten years ago and still being able to hear her voice, she was good. Until she began to really think about what just happened.

"I've been so stupid."

The clock had shown 10:40 pm which happened to be about five hours after she had sacrificed her entire body to her own husband in the chambers of their own master bedroom. They had made passionate love for an entire hour. Their activities extended from 4:00 to about 5:20 and he needed a Honey Blonde tonight?

"How could he do it? He begged me to stop. How could he do it again? So five hours and you are energizer bunny rabbit? Oh my God! "This time the tears fell harder. Her face swelled and her newborn began to cry hysterically. She had telephoned the nanny and she happily came to her rescue and brought her quiet spirit that comforted her. Now with the baby secure and the other children fast asleep she was able to let it all out into her feather downed pillows. She cried so much that she was tired of hearing herself so she ceased.

Sharon was alerted by a phone call one hour later from a close friend and spiritual counselor, Antoine Knight, whom he had called and threatened to "go away forever" if she didn't forgive him. She guessed the counselor had changed his unstable mind because within hours he appeared at her feet. He was begging for her forgiveness though she had no ready response. As far as she was concerned, there was nothing more to say. She was fat, he was a liar and her face was swollen. They had both made her ugly for three hours now. Really.....there was nothing left to say.

Since he was last fixated on killing himself, she figured it was better for him to decide his own fate seeing as though she didn't care. She was too busy fighting for her own sense of hope.

"Just kill us both then...this really really hurts...." She was still baffled by the five hour time window and the imprinted vision of her sitting in her barely there vehicle with the interior lights on, fluffing those damn Honey Blonde curls of hers while waiting for her "Mr. Tell Me Anything." All after congratulating her on their son's anticipated arrival just ten months prior at a game where she succeeded in touching her tummy while going on and on about how beautiful she was. It was too much for Sharon to bear. "How long has this been going on?"

"Yeah, I bet I *was* so beautiful." She was so beautiful that it didn't dawn on her that Miss Honey Blonde was creeping with her local celebrity on a pissed out mattress on the scummy floor of a townhouse with unlocked windows.

"You natural born slut! How dare she place her filthy hands on my tummy? "Sharon began to itch just thinking about it. "That girl touched me and tonight I touched *her* *ass* in such a way that she will never forget me. "

Sharon had one thing on her mind now............"What did I do to deserve this kind of pain? I have loved you with all of my heart and given you all the desires of your heart, known to me. I have listened intensely and I was happy to assist in making your dreams come true so many times. So why this, why her, why now? "

"Baby please let me say something before I go. I know you don't want to see my face but listen please. I love you more than I love my own life and I'm not gonna live without you. You are all I have. I told you that I'm nothing without you. Please, if you're gone, I don't want to live."

She listened on though her heart ached and her pride was compromised. There was something about Mr. Tell Me Anything that captured her each and every time he apologized. But this time was a little different.

"I'm sorry, I'll do anything. I won't make it another day if you leave me."

"So you'll do anything?"

"Anything!"

She laid down her request, "You *will* be going to church on every Sunday and you *will* be talking to Mr. Knight weekly and *you will not be* hanging out with nobodies all the time anymore. Tell them fools goodbye. No more mood enhancers, no more smoking and you know what else!"

"Okay, whatever you want me to do just don't leave me."

She quietly whispered, "Thank you God, now he can get better."

She kept a small piece of her to herself though, this time. "He will not be sleeping with me tonight or any other night until I want him too. If he needs some love, he'll have to get it from his fat girl until I am ready and by the looks of it and his lies that isn't going to be *anytime* soon."

It was the very first time he actually thought of her enough to eliminate the bad apples. Sharon closed her eyes and allowed her mind to sail forward to the day that he would get saved and delivered from his evil ways. Then she drifted further to her visit at the jewelers tomorrow. She had decided on a twelve karat tennis bracelet or a diamond tennis necklace. This fiasco would call for a little extra on his behalf.

"All his bitches are gonna break his ass. " Then she fell fast asleep before her heart burst or the condom resurfaced in her mind.......

159

CHAPTER 9
GLITTERBUG

She was all tucked into her California king comforter with her newborn at her side. Yes, she was a Mommy *again*. Sharon thought to herself that "maybe I should take her upstairs. I haven't made love to my husband in one whole day. "The two had just come out of an eleven month cleansing period, as they healed from all the scars and disappointments. This year was truly a year of love and affection towards one another. He loved to get in their rounds while he was in town. She was his opponent, he was the champ and she would let him beat it up every single chance she got. "Good Dick has healing powers, you know. "

Sharon kissed her baby on her rosy cheeks and decided it was time for Mommy and Daddy's rumble. "So off you go," as they headed up the long stairwell. She was careful not to wake her, being a professional mother now as she laid her gently into her crib. She released a small sigh and puckered her full lips outwardly as she settled into her own nursery where she had not spent many nights. But tonight there would be fireworks down in Mama's room, no place for an infant. Fire was hazardous.

She could hear the garage door go up and the Bentley pull in. Then down went the garage door and he began to tap the alarm code in. He was in now! In all the excitement her body was heated inside as she ran her fingers through her lap and propped her pillow up flinging the covers off quickly to get into position. She was all set now. He usually checked on his kids first, a new tradition after getting rid of the posse. So, she had at least two more minutes and if she was lucky he would be thirsty enough to stop in the kitchen for red Gatorade and look through the week's mail on the countertop. She needed a small delay to put lotion on her toes that she just looked down at. He didn't like ashy feet. "Now there.....I'm ready."

Sharon could hear his footsteps glide across the travertine floors. As he got closer, her heart began to race. They would kiss and she would undress him and all nine inches of his manhood and then he would slide right up inside of her. As his hand touched the doorknob she began to bite the left bottom corner of her lip. Then he entered dressed in a custom gray suit, gray gators and a lavender tie with designer shirt that he had already undone. He had gotten in an hour later than usual but normally she didn't keep up with the time because he was always stopping off to pick up things or hanging with his buddies outside of the plane. They had just begun their new "trust" rituals where "you are where you say you are." Besides, she needed the extra minutes to do her lotion ritual thing.

"Baby, how was your trip?"

"It was cool. I slept the whole way."

"Are you tired?"

"Not really."

That's all she needed to hear. She rose up beckoning him over to the edge of the bed and then began to madly kiss him. Sharon forced her wet tongue down the back of his widely open throat. He kissed her back a little harder than normal but she was all about newness and hardness. So it was on! Afterwards, as planned, she undressed herself and then him. She was very aggressive like that. As she suckled his stern neck and the corners of his hard bare chest, her eye caught it! First she frowned and then she pushed him away saying, "What is this?"

"What?"

"This."

"What?"

She shoved him in his back towards the bathroom, popped the switch and there it was now, more visible than ever in the bright 60 watt lights, lip gloss was on his chest.

"And don't play with me like I'm crazy because I know what lip gloss looks like. I ain't no fool."

"Baby what? We went in to the strip club for a quick minute and you're flipping out about that? You know I always go in the joint the last Friday of the month. Why you tripping?" He was right, today was the last Friday in the month. They had begun this whole "it's okay to see but not touch thing." Yes, they had lots of new rituals. She was willing to try anything to make her marriage work. "Okay, that was a close call. "In their lifestyle it was common for the crew to hang out at the strip joint at least once a month. Strippers were always known as "better than groupies" because they were supposed to be nastier. Many thought of them as nice to look at but too nasty to even think about touching. As crazy as it sounds......it never came across that way to Sharon. She would try anything to please him. So she apologized to him in her raspy voice saying,

"Baby, so did you see one that was fine as me? What about the chocolate one with the cherry tattoo on her lips?"

She was smiling, flirting and making her own senses heightened and then she realized he wasn't aroused. "What in the world have I done?"

She was flipping about the strip club and she had ruined their night. All the kids were sleep, her hormones were raging, her weight and her toned body were now perfect and she needed him tonight but there was no arousal. He laid down beside her and held her close until she needed to go the bathroom. She was in need of a cold shower and she decided to catch him in the morning. He was *always ready* in the morning. On the way out of the bathroom, she tripped over his shoes and custom suit on her way back to the bed as she listened to him snore. With insomnia now and active hormones she decided to pick up his belongings and place them in the dry cleaning basket. So, she did and to her surprise she spotted it. There was lip gloss all over the insides of his underwear. He had been given a head job!!! She went to her closet and observed the stains once again, this time in tears and 100 watt lighting.

"He is cheating." His suit smelled like cheap perfume and hot ass. While she thought it to be entertainment he had used it for other purposes. "How could he do this to us? How could he look me right in my face and lie to me? He just made a fool of me again. He let me blame myself.

Instead of him telling her anything, Sharon had graduated now to telling it all to herself. "How could he do this to me? Well we will just have to see. "

In the sweetest voice she had ever used she said, "Baby, can you wake up? I want to ask you something very important. Baby, why do you have glitter on your chest and glitter in your dras? If you had to get that done you could have got that done at the house. You know you really disgust me. But I'm not going to argue with you tonight. Your kids are asleep. I was really happy before you got here, so I'm not going to argue with you. I'm guessing you did what you did cause you *wanted to* do it. Now I'm going to do what *I* want to do because I want to. I'm going to let you stay here with *your* kids and I'm going out to do whatever I want to do with *whoever I want to do it with like you been doing all this time.* Mama likes head, too. And I might just wanna glaze the inside of somebody else's underwear."

She slammed the door behind after grabbing a pair of jeans and a top. She hopped into her convertible Mercedes and she was pulling off when,

"You ain't doing shit in that car *that I bought*." His horns were standing on top of his head now. "Yes I am. You damn right, you bought it and everything else in this bitch but it's still mine. Don't get it twisted. And in the morning, if I *feel* like it you're going to buy me something else for all your damn lies. Honey, you can pay them whores, so you're gonna continue to pay me and make it worth my while, too."

And she punched the pedal and sped off. As the car picked up speed so did her heart. This was her first real power move. She had never spoken to him in that manner before. He had finally made her feel, that she was not enough for him. Perhaps she could be of some service to another man whose life's desire was to have a beautiful woman capable of loving and freaking him. She could definitely handle that. But where would she find this man? "I know, at the gas station. Men are always harassing me there with their shiny sports cars and fresh haircuts. They just stop and stare and ask, can I give you my number? Often I just throw my head back and to say, *Boy Please*. But I will definitely look into changing this little ritual. Maybe, I should meet an older man. They seem to be a little more settled. But what is he going to do with me in bed? It takes a lot to handle my little wild ass. I would probably end up killing him from having to pop them *get your dick hard pills*. I couldn't possible do that to him. What about a white man? Yep, I'll trade races and see what benefits I can stumble upon. Yes, Master. I heard they eat vaginas much better than brothers. (That's always a plus) One thing for sure, I got a mouth full for him. And....... I heard they treat you better too. Imagine that, a black queen is a white man's dream. Damn, I never even thought of another man in all these years. The possibilities here are endless."

She got over twenty-five phone calls before she even left the subdivision. She was going to show his cheating ass. Then she finally answered because she was getting sick of him calling and sick of having multiple men in her head. She had gone from zero to whore in twenty five seconds flat.

"What?"

"Baby, listen."

"Listen to *what*, more of your lies tonight? That's okay, I'll see you and your checkbook in the morning."

Never before had she addressed him in that way. She was losing much respect for this individual and she was seeing other people in her mind now. She knew that mentioning his money would hurt him because he always thought that people were after it. Click, she hung up.

Sharon drove to her father's house. She would be safe there. She also knew that that would piss him off too. He hated other people being put into his business. In all her rages, she learned to use her words. They were her only defense. The man was a real giant. And Lord knows his hands felt like chains when he wrapped them around her little neck.

"His ass gonna buy me a helicopter tomorrow. "She had everything else already. Sharon laughed to cover her grief. She was getting pretty good at it, too.

He found her car at her dad's an hour later.... With his stalking ass. He rang the doorbell for three hours straight. "Forget him," she thought. "He's always done what he wanted to do but it has never affected our sex life. You can't take stuff out of my house down to the whore house. He's crazy. I'm so done with this situation."

Something inside of her blocked the actual act of what he had done and fast forwarded to what he didn't do. She wasn't gonna suffer anymore loss for anybody. She needed what she needed when she needed it and she was going to get it. He was going to get out the way and turn his position over to someone else, someone who could be trusted.

"I'm not a girl who likes to be at the mercy of any man or woman and I do not like to be put on hold. I want mine. My hormones are raging and you've taken my partner over to a club and let a stranger suck the life out of him. Oh hell no, I'm going to bed. The next time he touches me he's going to be past ready because he's gonna be feigning for this. I'm not going to let him as much as smell it for the next month. He will go crazy for sure. Damn him, let the games begin...... And he better hope that I don't run into anything worthwhile at that damn gas station."

Sharon returned home after eleven days. She began calling him glitterbug every time he begged for it. She would say, "Naw, I don't sleep with glitterbugs."She was torturing his ass with lingerie morning, noon and night. She didn't have a career thus far but now she would start one up. She would be a lingerie model. Yes and their house would be her runway. Every corner that he turned, she was half naked, all day long..... Morning, noon, and night. To make matters worse she was very kind to him, offering him home cooked meals and lots of empty advice. Her mother always said, *kill them with kindness*.

After three additional weeks, he began to get very angry, but she wasn't going to let up for anything. This one particular night she was almost raped by exiting the shower and purposely taking twenty minutes to dry, twenty minutes to put on perfumed oils and twenty minutes practicing *I'm so sexy sound effects* in the mirror. She had this man going. He was drooling at the mouth.

Sharon thought to herself, "where is his stripper now? I guess it hadn't been such a great blowjob after all. "And her clothes got tighter, the weave got longer and her voice got sweeter. He was losing it. She needed him to feel all of her pain.

Finally, after five weeks of this madness he breaks out with a diamond Rolex watch saying he was just thinking about how much she meant to him and he wanted her to have it. Her first reaction was to slap his face at his insinuation that she would be bought with a price. But she didn't want to seem too ungrateful either. Her dad always said, *stay humbled* so she let him touch her wrist while he slid it on her.

"Damn, his hands feel like perfect gloves after frost bite. I miss him." She held her ground.

"So, what else you got?"

Then he laughed for the first time in over a month, threw her down upon their bed of frustrations and lies and tormented her body the way she had tormented his mind for weeks. As she released her frustration over and over again the glitter started to fade. All she could see now more vividly than ever was his face. So she climbed on top of it and placed something very special in his mouth. It was the one thing he was good at right from the beginning, without having to tell her anything.

Tonight there would be no more lies. The truth was perfectly clear. Her body had overruled her heart once again. As she surrendered her body over to her husband, she felt *dirty f*or the first time. Because as the orgasms came over and over again, she had imagined that she was someone else. All the faces from the gas station flashed before her. Sharon Roberson screwed half of Memphis, Atlanta and Los Angeles tonight....*what a bad little girl.* And he never even noticed. Ha! He had believed the moaning was a result of his provided services....like it had been so many times before. But, not tonight.

"It's funny how men think that they can do it *all* and think that your little silly self is gonna be *always there* to take it all in. I'm not quite brave enough to see another man, but I will *wish* him into our bed and he will live in *my head* for now. The danger and thrill of him should assist us both right now. I can't even have an orgasm without him around right now. It's pretty bad...I admit. But Rolex or not, you left Kitty unattended while you flaunted your whores around. So deal with it. You better be glad that I found her some invisible company. The real kind *is* just down the street at the gas station.....waiting."

CHAPTER 10
THE RENEWAL

It was almost dark outdoors, Sharon could see the hues change as the darkness hovered and yielded to the glory of the landscaped sky. It was an amazing sight to behold. As she stood starring into her evening of love, a gentle breeze brushed past her made up face. Its strength could have possibly been a lot stronger but with a ton of foundation on, she had to give an estimate only.

She held on to the rail on the balcony while reminiscing about how Mr. Tell Me Anything had asked her to marry him again. At first she thought it was somewhat silly because they hadn't been divorced.... They were just sleeping in separate beds for three consecutive months. It seemed like much longer to them both. But time and love expedited this night of renewal and it was going to be perfect for them. They needed this fresh start. She would be his wife "for real" this time.

The new coordinator was wonderful and very knowledgeable about all the local venues. Because of her expertise, they had selected her. She had come highly recommended as the mother of another local celebrity. Mrs. Hemmington was very classy and precise. So there was nothing for the couple to do but sit back, relax, and write checks while she basically handled *everything*.

"I had no idea that it would be this beautiful at sunset.....Oh my Lord....it's breath taking."

"Yes it is."

It was in the Ballroom located on the top floor of a prestigious world class restaurant, with a huge lookout of the entire city with lights. It was fabulous. The couple had decided to be "on top" of things this time around. And they were.

The past year had been filled with so many trials. The last fiasco had proven to be devastating enough to make them both separate, although they continued to live under the same roof for the sake of the kids and the coaching staff. Sharon was always careful not the ruin her husband's image. She had gotten comfortable with her "faking" until he gave in, coming home and pledging his new commitment to do "whatever it took" to make them work.

Once a week, they would host a Bible Study at their house with their spiritual mother and father. They would spend hours and hours with the Lord in prayer. Sharon had to admit that it was a little strange having him around so much. At times, it was wearing her down, but she had no complaints. She didn't want to interrupt the new healing process that seemed to be taking place. She had changed as well. The friends didn't even bother anymore. Most of them ran away so to speak. Demons didn't like Bible Study......they only liked free drugs and drama. Her suffocating days were over.

"No more goody bags.........so no more friends. Thank you, Jesus."

Today was just a day of celebration. Altogether, it was the day that she could officially lay aside all the weight that had easily beset her in the past from the very start. It was a day of love and laughter. She had learned to laugh all over again....she was free in God.

"I'm free indeed."

She wasn't concerned about the overdone arrangements or the cuisine....she just wanted to hear him say some new things to her that really meant something this time. She also had the opportunity to buy a new dress. And it was gorgeous. Although it was a size fourteen and had a baby bulging from underneath it.....it was simply extravagant.

The new baby just kind of popped up as a result of making up for all the years of pain. But they both wanted it so bad because the loss of their daughter had been too much for them both. This one would also be a girl. Now the couple could start over in two detrimental areas where they needed help the most...........parenting and love.

Though it was exquisite, the ceremony was well within their budget because they didn't have one. There was not a price ticket on fixing all of his lies and deceit that had already cost him practically everything.

Sharon had a *new* man now. He had learned from the counselors to "share." So, now she got the chance to hear all the amusing stories about all the treacherous women and whatever else he needed to get out of his head. The decisions about their future were starting to be made by them *both* with honest means. They were a real couple now. Their life was like an episode of the Brady Bunch. It was a dream for her. She loved him more than ever now.

As the months passed, she wasn't bored, but she was looking for a drama here and there to keep her going. So, she spent time trying to conjure up meaningless arguments. He never subscribed to them though. He knew her way to well for that.....always exclaiming..."Baby come on...you ain't *that* mad *about that*." Sharon thought that maybe he was boring her on purpose for some cruel payback. She was losing her mind in the blissfulness. Nevertheless, it was great for the children. They had no grumbling at all. They loved him being around all the time.

The music was playing softly, but Sharon could hear it aloud as it was soothing to her soul. It was tuned in to all their love songs selected by them both and played by her baby brother, Terrell. Each song had meant something special, like a milestone at a particular time in their recovery process. It was truly flawless.

Sharon was filled with joy as she commanded her heart, "Don't burst before I get the chance to marry him again." She thought of all they had conquered. She remembered the fire and the rain. "We need this and our children deserve this." They would renew their love with everyone present this night.

The romantic and intimate evening would take place shortly in the decorated Ballroom but not before she would think back to the first wedding "Half our guests were strangers." She was glad they could get a do over and just have important individuals involved this time. And they were all there ready with their cameras. Her friends wanted it more than ever for them. They had felt the two were destined to be together forever.

Outside in the hallway she caught a glimpse of him and their four sons. They were snapping numerous photographs with their photographer and friend, Monte. He was bad!!!! He could even make her appear skinnier if she wanted..."yes." They had chosen him because not only did he have a way with poses but their kids loved him as well.

Sharon couldn't help it. She slid back into her dressing station and cried. "My God...you have blessed us so much this year. I give you all the honor and glory for today and this new life that I have. I love him and I thank you from the bottom of my heart. Help us to continue to grow together." She had learned how to pray now through their counselor. After her praise moment, her closest friends and two sisters were standing in front of her. Technically one was her real sister and the other, Cousin Claudette, who you couldn't tell the difference. They both loved her the same. They were her strength at times. "Are you okay?"

"Yeah, just having a moment."

"If he doesn't do right this time, we're gone *have us* a moment."

"Give him a chance…..he's different now."

"Okay…………I guess we will see. I'll give him three months."

"Come on…..don't say that."''

"Okay….I'm just saying, girl."

Maybe she was right somehow, but Sharon believed in him. She believed in the *new* things that he had said. He was much different now. He was finally coming into himself as a father and good man.

"Do you remember what you are going to say?"

Sharon looked at her daughter and smiled. She was her only girl now with one more on the way to greet them both and even out the hormones in the house full of testosterone. She had volunteered to do a dance in her parents' honor. How sweet it was to have a daughter who wanted to be an intricate part of their day. She was Sharon's spitting image with green eyes and perfect teeth. She was everything to them both…….especially her father. She had him twisted around her finger with her rosy little cheeks and raspy voice.

"How does mommy look?"

"You look *really* pretty."

"Thank you, baby."

Sharon loved her more than words could ever express. But this day she would be escorted by her oldest son down the aisle....her dad had passed away now. He too died from cancer. "He would have been proud of you, Mommy."

"I know, baby."

She and her son had a bond like no other mother and son she knew. He was her biggest fan always asking her question after question. He wanted to know everything. And today he knew one thing for sure....his Mommy was beautiful and she and his dad would be Happily Ever After again.

"All ready?"

And they started down the aisle. Mr. Tell Me Anything stood waiting for his clean slate and their new beginning. This time they were solid and ready.

There they stood before God and all their witnesses and shared their written vows one at a time:

His: "Baby, I know we've been through a lot together. Well, basically I put you through a lot. And you have stood beside me through everything. But today my promise is that I am going to be the husband that you always wanted me to be ...the kind of husband you deserve. Our love is forever. I'm not gonna let you or the kids down this time...I'm nothing without you."

They weren't rehearsed…..Sharon was without words. Hers were a little simpler in nature. She gathered that they could be since she was the faithful one who had taken all his crap. Yet still she didn't want to say the wrong thing in her response or reply.

She treaded lightly in the complete silence….

Hers: "Today I want to be your wife again. I thought I was happy the first time you asked me, but today I realize that you have made me happier than ever, today. I love you and our kids so much and I will forever. I'm thankful for what we have."

And it was over. They had told each other everything and they were together again forever.

CHAPTER 11
MISS FIFTEEN HUNDRED

All of a sudden, Sharon was perched in her tiny piece of a living room on a neutral colored contemporary sofa near the front door. She was waiting eagerly for her to appear from the hidden stairwell from what seemed to be the convenient love nest. It was neatly decorated, furniture, not too expensive, so that was always a plus. At least he didn't spend all of their family fortune on his mistresses. As a matter of fact, Sharon had learned from several ambitious friends, foes and from her own personal investigations that Mr. Tell Me Anything only dispensed her Fifteen Hundred Dollars per month to live on. With a bulging salary like his and excessive allowance like hers, surely a measly Fifteen Hundred dollars was scraps for the countless lonely nights that she must have had too often endure. He was always with his wife and their kids. Sharon had made sure of it herself due to his background of lies and deceit. She could remember one of their part time nannies, Ms. Brenda, as she offered her advice....." You can't stop him, girl but you can sholl slow him down." It was the best advice she had received that particular year.

He also traveled way too much and spent hours and hours with his leaching posse. So when did he have an opportunity to spend any quality time with this female? And if she was even worth babbling about, why would she settle for anything less than $5000 a month.

"What can you buy with Fifteen Hundred in Atlanta, Georgia? " Sharon had begun to feel sorry for her and her preposterous situation.

Then she appeared with a petite nicely built frame. There was nothing distinctive to brag about but definitely nothing comical about her presence either. Her stressed brown shoulder length hair was all over her head, not to mention she needed a perm like that day(hour). What's funny though is that her complexion was for all practical purposes very similar to Sharon's. Though her skin resembled hers in color, she was a twist between Asian African and Indian African.

"Okay, this girl has some great skin."

Her only apparent flaw would be her inadequate height, standing only 5'4" tall. This was definitely a handicap. He liked giving it to her standing from behind.

"What in the hell was he thinking? How could he get a midget reject to make him feel good and destroy my life at the same time? "

Sharon had heard from several people ·that she screwed several players on the way to hers. No one had fallen for her bullshit because she was a "party girl" with no "class" about herself. She was just a whore with smooth sounding words.

"How sweet? A Mr. and Miss Tell Each Other Anything……. Classic."

But Sharon was on top of things. Back in detective mode, she began asking questions about her from the start. She had inquired about the way they met and was told she readily offered her assistance with an online degree program and he had marveled at the chance. She had enticed him with her devious mind and her special offers. And she had definitely succeeded. Sharon had to admit that she was a little worried about this one now because she was his first *smart side piece*. All of a sudden she wasn't just his next victim of circumstance awaiting her very brief dismissal. She had taken on an altogether new role. It started to seem as though she was sort of a token to him. This was a *new show*, starring his new educated clear complexion whore. She no longer made the comparison to any of her previous contenders. She was somewhat "special," this girl. And to make matters more crucial……. She was a whole five years younger than Sharon. He always told his wife that he loved older women.

"Yeah right, just tell me anything. "

Miss Fifteen Hundred, if patient could eventually become a smaller version of herself. He loved a woman with book sense. In high school, Sharon did all of his homework and maintained an A average. For decades she had believed he would never find another woman in this world with the beauty and brains that she possessed. From High School, she graduated as an honor student at the top of her class. She was offered several full academic scholarships due to her extremely high GPA and several others because of her above average ACT score. Life was good. She could have been anything that her heart imagined because her brain had always done overtime when it came to studies. But tragedy had given her life the biggest blow ever known to a young woman…..the death, burial and complete loss of her mother. She had no choice but to quit and spend her last waking moments at her side.

Someone once said, "You should live your life without regrets," Sharon thought to herself. "Why do I have so many right now?"

Her head was bombarded by the thought now that he himself had insisted on her quitting school to raise their children. She wondered how he could work secretly to receive his degree with the assistance of this smart tramp, while he shoved her goals aside.

"What a Bastard!!! "

But just when she thought this couldn't get any better, here he goes again.

"You shut down my life, only to continue pursuing yours and all your dreams? Baby Please. Give me some breathing room here. Let me come up for some air first."

It was difficult enough to sacrifice all her time to motherhood. She would spend every waking moment with all of them, him included.

"Now you want to add this in? What do you expect me to do? Oh okay, so I'm supposed to sit idly by while you and Miss Fifteen Hundred engage in intellectual conversations about fascinating things like your damn degree. My choices are to converse with at least six candidates under the age of ten. Lord have mercy."

She found him to be selfish and ridiculous.

"You have got to be the most selfish bastard I have laid eyes upon. "

This had not been blackmail as her twisted mind had perceived it before. This crap they had was underlined with substance. She had it all thought out now.

And then she finally spoke, "I knew this day was coming."

"Oh so you did? So why in God's world didn't anyone inform me about it? "

Nobody had called her. Nobody had told her anything. She's in the dark attending to her newborn baby, again. She had a one month old now. He has her rocking babies, changing diapers, and breastfeeding while he is at the convenient love nest with Miss Educated Fifteen Hundred.

Again she spoke her self-proclaimed prophecy, "I knew this day was coming."

This time Sharon was tuned in to the six excruciating words that pierced her ears as she was getting really pissed off. If she wasn't on her way to being saved she would have known just how angry she was, but her mother always said, "Remain a lady at all times." (Deep Breath)

"So you knew he was married?"

And she responded, "Yes, but he told me that you guys were separated. This is a big mistake."

"Oh, he did? Is that right?"

This lying female knew he was coming home every night. She thought they were separated? How are they separated and every morning they wake up together. It is amazing the lengths groupies go to.

Now Sharon is really losing it. She realizes that he actually talks to her. She thought this was like a drive by love nest. People actually get together in this tiny place, sleep together, talk about her and lie on her while she is at home rocking babies. Something was about to get snatched off her wall or the hair out of her head or those Louis Vuitton bags...............

"Oh, my God, she has Louis Vuitton under her freaking Christmas tree? "

Sharon had lost all train of thought at this point. She had gotten Louis Vuitton? This man has gone crazy! It ain't nothing in Louis Vuitton under Fifteen Hundred Dollars. Not a belt, not a buckle, not a bag, not anything in that store under Fifteen Hundred!!!!!! Her budget had just gone up. Some major lies had been told here. He had better........then he called.

He already knew she was there. Their personal trainer had known she was there also so he gave him the courtesy of a personal phone call, them being such good friends and all. And he had taken her oldest daughter, home, her being in the car and all. She had navigated her mommy's turn because her father had taken her there just the day before. He told her he was checking on a place for his friend to live. There is nothing more serious than drafting kids into your schemes. Sharon was on her way to the mall when her little voice whispered, "Mommy, we went this way yesterday." She had led her to her destiny.

Sharon pulled up at the love nest and spotted the trainer's truck, fixating her eyes on his Tennessee tags in Georgia and the undeniable scratch on the back of the truck's bed. As she glanced around, she witnessed him coming out of her residence. She jumped out and asked about his being there. He had told her what seemed to be the truth but who cared? He knew her. Yes, he was bringing medicine because she was not feeling well per Mr. Tell Me Anything's instructions. Her first thought was what kind of medicine?

"Whatever she has I probably have contracted it too at this point. We are sharing the same man. For God's sake, I hope she ain't sick *for real*." Sharon began to feel nauseated. It crashed down on her like an enormous boulder. She started feeling the weight of being such an idiot with every breath that she breathed in. Her lungs were filled with total despair.

"I Give Up. This is too much. Now he's her freaking caretaker?"

Sharon could remember the last time she was sick. She had to spend a fortune to fly her stepmom in town because he was "too busy" in training camp. He hadn't even attempted to come to her rescue.

"Who cares if she needed medical attention?" Her mind was discombobulated by the fact he even knew her.

"Did the entire posse know her too?"

She was thrown back in time again. He was up to his same ole crap. What seemed like a small amount of quality time started to suddenly turn into a well-known relationship. It was a relationship known by others as well as her son who opened the door for her. What a nice young man he seemed, inviting her inside with no questions asked, strange little Sharon Roberson. Their trainer had agreed to take their daughter home in order to keep her out of the line of fire and to give his buddy a phone call. The son had agreed to place his mom in an awkward situation today where she would have to face the wife once and for all.

"What nice people there are in this world?"

As she stumbled over her words, grasping for more lies, Sharon began to see why they might be the perfect fit. There were both so eloquent with words. Someone should have named them Mr. and Mrs. Liar. She scrambled for more as she snagged a seat on the sofa across from her.

"Brave Girl," she thought. "God I'm going to need you. "

There was only one small coffee table dividing the two of his women. She had to look away to collect her thoughts when she noticed there was no television in the area where they were sitting. And being a townhouse, the convenient love nest did not possess a den or hearth room either. These two types of rooms generally cost over Fifteen Hundred Dollars a month. Simultaneously, she could hear a television show playing from one of the bedrooms upstairs. So they didn't just sit here and look at each other on these cheap ass sofas and nobody has ever sat at that poor excuse for a dining table over there. The back door could be seen from the front door in this shotgun home.

"So you must be spending all of your time up in your room!! Hell Naw! "

Sharon was raised in the heart of the hood. It was in her blood two days out of the week and she had no desire to change who she was whether she was in arm's reach or not.

First she thought, "Go upside this bitch's head," then she began to think "So Fifteen Hundred a month gets you television shows upstairs in her bedroom? Wow this is getting better and better."

She was starring in his *new show* with his cheap whore. Her new faith was wavering a bit. But after intermission....... the unthinkable happened....... Mr. Tell Me Anything called her cell phone and Miss Fifteen Hundred responded, "She's right here."

"What the hell? Wait a freaking minute, this lying son of a bitch is asking about me? Why didn't he call *my* phone?" But she said it in silence.

I guess her expression landed somewhere in between awe hell naw and awe hell to da naw because Miss Fifteen Hundred proceeded in placing him on speakerphone while gesturing Sharon to be quiet. She didn't like the bullshit but it was her house (townhouse) and she wanted to know everything. Free information was always a plus. Private investigators can dissolve a college fund. This was gonna be the day he was going to answer to all of his lies and save her some money and precious time. Somebody was going to explain to her.

The leading actor started his script, "Why is she still there?"

She was trying so desperately to explain. They were communicating so easily that it seemed so natural for the both of them. It was so naturally done that you couldn't tell who his wife was and who the imposter was. It was as if she was Sharon and Sharon was her for a tiny moment. She had even called him by his nickname? In the past, she had deceived herself into thoughts like these women were stalking him. She always allowed him to take on the role of the ultimate victim. Most times, if they called him by nickname, it would make her infuriated because she felt they had no right. Often, she would convince herself to believe they somehow retrieved this personal information from the internet. Everything was always everybody else's fault. He was never to blame.

But this day, he was not a potential victim at all. He was the ring leader and she was his circus clown. They had only lived in the Atlanta area for four months. Four months, Fifteen Hundred dollars and she was calling Mr. Tell Me Anything by his nickname?

"God, you gotta help me now. This is moving way too fast for me."

Sharon thought of the fifteen hundred dollars and that it was all that this prostitute deserved. She understood his sporadic nature and his flaws but this was different than all the other times. Somehow she began viewing this drive through as a dine-in type of place. All in all she remembered her mother's dying plea for sophistication so she rose to the occasion and decided to listen peacefully on. She wanted to be precise and somewhat brave this time. They had been through too much together. It was time to be a *big girl* about this one. She paced her own heartbeat and opened her mouth, "My God, we have a newborn baby girl." She was so precious to him. She even resembled him and his mother even though the grandma had only laid eyes on her once in her little lifetime (but that's another story). It never bothered Sharon though. She was well prepared for her neglect issues seeing she had not mothered her own son. She had no expectations when it came to his people now. Her goal was only to have Mr. Tell Me Anything do what was right. Surely, this was not a mistake. And with her remarkable resemblance Sharon had thought God to have a sense of humor…..something she could use at this moment.

His voice emerged again, "Well, if someone was at *my* house and *I* wanted them gone, *I'd call the police.*"

"What? Did he just say what I heard him say?" She was crushed.

All her delusions were valid reasons to walk away from this scene and this very mortifying situation. Inside she began to weep and on the outside her previous "he's mine" expressions immensely softened.   All her mind could do was drift back to the day she was laid out on the floor of their Georgia mansion. How did she get there? He had struck her so hard that gravity had taken its role. So, there she was, children all present, laying face up with a head concussion. All she could feel was the warmth of her own tears trickling down behind her ears as they filled up the travertine tile floors in puddles. Mind you, he had only struck her three times before that. But neither of his previous offenses ended with her hitting the ground. They all did have one thing in common though…..they started with his infidelity coming to light. But the night she hit the stony floor was different. The violence had escalated. In fact, it was so different she had thought only to escape when she was capable of standing to her feet. She thought to "leave for good" after he left for his road trip of course. But she guessed her expression was a dead giveaway because he called in to work. No one she knew in professional basketball had ever done that before. Who does that in his field? What employee calls their boss in order to stand guard at their own home? First he hit her, and then he held her hostage? All and all she remembered laying there for several moments in agonizing pain. She could only imagine what the kids were thinking as they saw him strike her. Sharon could remember their whimpering sobs and their distraught little faces. Would this affect them in a negative way? Often he had told her that his mother had beaten him as a child. And this was the reason custody was given over to his Grandmother. Was he destined to be just like her? Should she bail? If she left would he come after her? She didn't even say anything to make him that mad. She grew up all this time thinking that if she kept quiet, a man would have no reason to strike her. Her Daddy only lashed out when her Mama's words had gotten too fierce.

So why did *he* do it? Was this life too much for him to handle? She was only asking about the number that came across his two-way and why it was always buzzing at the most inappropriate times. She knew he hated when she asked him questions, so she even checked her tone and approach. Her brother always told her that if a man is reluctant to answer questions he was probably hiding something. But there was nothing you could tell her about *her* man. And besides, he was too busy telling her everything himself. Lord knows she had believed him even from the floor. She needed to believe that he felt as much pain as she was feeling. He had said he was "sorry" and that he would never do it again. He also uttered that she had *made him do it* with her calm disposition. He had said that she had appeared "*not to care*" because she didn't subscribe to going back and forth with him. That is what they did before marriage and it always ended with him snatching her arm. She was tired of hiding the bruises from her family. Besides, she had no time to argue over every little detail. It was time to grow up. The more he spoke, the more unrealistic he had seemed anyway. She thought silence was golden for them. But she obviously had more to learn. Nonetheless she had never ever let her mind travel to thought of calling the cops on him. She would never place him in a bind like that. She was placed in his life for protection and love. He had enough people that had betrayed and deserted him. So, she vowed to be different. Yes, it was all up to her to give him what he never had, security. She could not possibly accomplish that with the local police in their business or the vicious news team at their front door. So, she endured the pain and covered his indiscretions for years and years. No one would understand that he was only a product of his previous environment. Changing him over would take more time. There was no love anywhere around him, only individuals with their hidden agendas. But what was clear to Sharon was that they had damaged him, child abuse was such an awful thing. It had messed up his mind. And he had needed more than a part time father to lick his wounds. He needed someone there to let him know that he was really loved and that he really mattered to them. His thighs would remind him each time he showered of being beaten by a bullwhip. Who would do such a thing to their own flesh and blood? Sharon had tried not so desperately to hate them both, *her* for striking him and *him* for living in a whole different state and not even knowing or caring what was being done to him. His was a scar that would never leave. So she committed herself to concealing it with *her* new found physical wounds. Now no one would ever know his pain, or hers. No figure of authority was gonna be allowed to place him in the backseat of their ride. She loved him way too much for that.

"So why would he say that? Why would he sail me up the river just like that?"

Before she hung up the telephone, the Spirit had given Sharon peace and kind words to express. Miss Fifteen Hundred looked over at the vexed wife and began to explain how he had lied to her. Before she allowed the natural liar to elaborate any further, Sharon began to minister with her mouth slightly opened. God allowed her purposely muffled words to be heard as she lifted her arched eyebrows.

"You're not a bad looking girl. I am so sorry about this; he *has* been lying to you. But now you're lying to me. You knew there was no separation, there wasn't any talk of separation, no thought of separation and he happens to love me very much. If he didn't he would more than just drive by here, get free favors and roll out after throwing you some pathetic little fifteen hundred dollar check and a few sweet innuendos. Don't you think you're worth more than that?" She didn't really see how she could see it because she couldn't see it either, but it was a nice thing to say. She was trying to help them both out.

Imagine that, trying to get Miss Fifteen Hundred to acknowledge that Mr. Tell Me Anything who pays *her* bills and watches *her* cable television upstairs in *her* bedroom loves her *and only her*.

A NOTE FROM THE WISE:

Don't try this at home, it doesn't work without God. She had tried it a couple of times before and it ended miserably. When you are not grounded in God you can forget trying to handle the other woman. It's too much pain there. The situation only gets worse without HIM. Besides the only person that believes in you and your self-proclaimed love is you. You cannot

convince someone who is picking up a monthly check and having
frequent rumbles in the bedroom with your man that first of all
he is yours. Then, second of all, how can you proclaim that he
loves you and only you. Furthermore, most other women are not
seeking status, they are seeking whatever they can get there
measly hands unto at that present time.

Sharon had perceived he was hers up until this point.

"I can't breathe."

She also perceived that he had tasted her cum, for sure.
Because the wise also say that mistresses are like spare
wives without the miles on them. When they get too
overused, they usually become even more like the wives
when he finds the latest edition of you both. Nonetheless,
her current position allowed for a huge piece of stock in
her husband. What her man couldn't give in time, he
probably provided in the bedroom. "What a disaster!" He
was definitely chewing her up on a regular basis. Nobody
sticks around for two years with a man who makes over a
million U.S. Dollars a month just to receive $1500 on the
side if she ain't being serviced properly. She's definitely
cumming in his mouth every chance she gets.

"Damn!"

Sharon could not find any other reasoning in her
participation in a two year old fling. This girl was still
someone to be highly considered now. He had actually
considered her. It was in her face now, too.......Like it was
before. But she had failed to accept it.....thinking it was

merely a joke and that her pain would propel him to push her aside like all the others. But Nooooooooo…he had to keep this one.

"I can't breathe."

All she desired was a clear exit to her luxury car with its tinted windows and stylish rims. Lord knows on this day she had needed them. She had needed the elusive darkness of the windows to camouflage her tarnished emotions. She had needed the brilliant rims as a distraction to fellow drivers who pulled up beside her. But most of all she needed God in all of his fullness to guide her vehicle to safety. She began to think of her husband as a trick of some sort or a teller machine. She could feel her love for him being stricken with grief, pain, and resentment. She just recently had another child at his request, now there were six of them.

"Lord, please help me and my babies."

The tears began to pour downward. They fell in puddles, in pools. They tumbled from the Lenox Mall to their Sandy Springs mansion. They had filled up her Range Rover. She could smell them mixed with the fresh leather of her customized seats. What could she say or did she say anything at all? How would she face him? How could he face her? No more lies, no more disguises, the jury was out, and his verdict was in. He had lied over and over again. Like the time she had caught him on the phone so elated that she thought he had renewed his contract or she was getting a new piece of jewelry. But in actuality he had been conversing with Miss Fifteen Hundred and she excited him to a point where he lost all train of thought and all sense of carefulness. In such a brief moment, his infatuation was unveiled but he quickly caught it when Sharon had walked out to his Cadillac Escalade in which he was sitting and talking right outside of their home.

This one girl she had designated as special because her name had rang on too many occasions, all incidents unresolved and left to her vivid wounded wife's imagination. So how was he going to explain this one? She had confronted her. She had been to her home. He had purchased Louis Vuitton, no lies now. No lies, she was not the educated aid assigned to him by his employer, Sharon had talked to her. She was not a friend of a friend who seemed so excited at your game; the wife had talked to her.

"How could he have lied so much? "

He often had told her that he would die without her and this was his day of reckoning. She was interested to see what approach he would take or what door she was going to kick him out of, all the while intending to let Miss Fifteen Hundred assist him with his packing. She definitely wanted him gone.

"He is getting the hell out today! Come on with your suicide threats, but that ass is getting out my house today."

In all the chaos, his countless lies had afforded him the courtesy of leaving work earlier than usual, because in all of her agony, he appeared. Sharon asked God to immediately cover her mind and bridle her tongue and it worked for the first ten minutes.

But she kept looking at him and thought of all she had invested. She thought of all he was willing to lose over a woman who he had just met. Suddenly, she wanted him to be with his "party girl." She wanted him to see what it was like without a "good woman" standing behind him in total submission and support. She wanted him to have a "real" gold digger so he could look back and feel as stupid as she did at the moment. He had lied way too much for this companion. She could not put them all in chronological order at this point. There were way too many of them swarming around in her head.

"Look, what are we gonna do? You have lied for whatever reasons. You've been too blessed to act this way. Be the man you're called to be. She's not worth losing everything! But if it's what you choose, I will get out of your way. I don't have a problem with it right now. I'm tired. You can have it. I need my peace back. You can have this life. Ever since you started making this money.... You have changed.... I like the old husband I had. This new person I don't know and to be quite honest I find myself afraid of him. Let's just go our separate ways. I promise.....I'm good with it. I'll just go back home to Memphis....we will let you be all that you can be here.......alone."

"No.....I just need to get myself together baby, I'm so sorry, I don't ever want to lose you and my kids, please forgive me. It's gonna take time. I'm really trying this time. I am so much better, you have no idea. I was just trying to get my degree, that's all."

She didn't proclaim it from the mountaintop but she had already forgiven him out of fear. Was she strong enough to raise six small children alone? It had not been the easiest task even with all the hired hands involved. She felt that kids really needed their parents....the kind of individuals who have clear minds to see after them. Would his pain be too much for her? Would they be better off without her as the weak woman she now exemplified? She didn't even know herself right now. She only existed in bits and pieces.

"Don't they deserve a *strong* Mommy who can put their interests first? What in the hell am I doing? I can't......I'm sorry I just can't" Her thoughts waved back and forth thinking about subjecting them to divorce....."They'll suffer even more at the hands of his sluts and mistresses. Hell, No!"

It was not going to be a walk in the park, but her and her jeans could do this! She pulled them further up into her creases and chose to become a walking display of how to show a man that he can't break you. She fell out laughing at her pitiful self, contemplating on NOT leaving and continuing on a shipwreck waiting to happen. But it was funny, she was her own joke.

"Damn girl, you funny as hell with your weak ass." She laughed again.

Sharon thought of the bridge downtown this time, a perfect place to end the jokes. So she laughed harder. It was either laugh or drive fast and jump. She decided to laugh louder and stay her little suicidal ass away from her hometown with all its death temptation. Her mind was too unstable for lighted bridges. So, she laughed on. It was not because of his words or their ongoing history; it was merely because she needed to. For the first time, she was vulnerable with six children to raise alone. She was afraid and they were wide-eyed with respect and admiration for the "family" they were proud to be a part of. For years, she had hid all his indiscretions behind her Louis Vuitton and Chanel bags. She was always thought to look "so happy." If she left tonight, she would be her Mama all over again. This was her greatest fear of all. She raised her and her siblings alone after going through hell and eventually losing her Daddy. He was the only true love of her life. After her loss of love, her broken heart would lead her stressed body to a bed of sickness and death. She was diagnosed with an aggressive form of breast cancer. The doctor said that her emotions possibly blocked her healing process. She died with her broken heart; that still longed for him despite their divorce. He landed in the arms of another woman, yet she had never let go of him. Was Sharon to be the same? She had already lost so much. As much as she admired her tenacity and quest for love, she was not willing to replay history, though. Or was she already on her way to doing that?

CHAPTER 12
RIDE OR DIE CHIC

"Sir, can you stop here for just a second, I'll be right back out."

"Yes, mam, no problem. I'm on YOUR time."

Sharon sat eagerly on the edge of the bench seat with her chin up, chest out and red bottoms intact, ready to flaunt her fire red polished toes to match. He would definitely be seduced by the vibrant toes; she had the self-indulgent habit of flashing her perfect feet towards lighted areas that initiated immediate male eye contact.

"For some reason men seem to love pedicured toes."

The normal routine would include a slight stare that was followed by a lingering eye that voyaged up her elongated legs that ended somewhere near her inner thighs. It was clear that they could sense that she never wore panties. Honestly, she don't even really own but three pairs.

"Who has time for panties? They are awfully restricting."

Her limo driver would soon discover her little secret. Panties weren't the only thing missing from her wardrobe tonight underneath the full-length mink coat. Sharon Roberson was *butt ass-naked.*

She was really not as perverse as it seems. At least she waited until the aircraft landed to undress. As they reached the gate in Ohio, her skin felt ultimately trapped inside the tiny maxi dress she was originally wearing. Her initial plan was to wear it until she could find a decent place to discard it. But there was no such place in the First-class cabin. Besides, the ventilation rendered lasting bursts of extreme air that required some covering on her behalf. As soon as she exited the plane, she made a sprint for the ladies' room and off it went....straight into her deep pocket inside the coat. After maneuvering out of the *freakum-dress*, her mission was clearer than ever.

"No time for clothing, I haven't seen my husband in eight whole days. It's on!!!!!"

His manhood was all she needed to see. He and she were well acquainted, with a very special relationship. Even when Mr. Tell Me Anything and Sharon were at odds with one another, *he* and *she* got along better than ever. He was their third party and mediator with a mind of his own. She loved him with all of her heart. At times, she began grasping the concept that he was the one she *really* married. He was the one that never changed on her. He had done so much for her....no lies....... just the two of them face to face. They belonged together. He always knew what she needed and was happy to deliver. What a combination for success!!!

"The dick and the damsel!" Sharon laughed out loud.

The mission became even clearer as the moments passed by.

"It's time to drop momma something off to get me through the next weeks to come. I'm in need!!! I can't wait!!!!!"

Her body commenced to break out in chill bumps and her nipples became erect at the thought of his touch. Sharon trembled.

"Mam, are you still going inside?"

"OMG!"

She had totally forgotten that he was standing outside the door with his hand extended to assist her.

"I'm sorry, I'll be right back."

She peeped back at the driver, trying to interpret whether he'd seen her vagina or not. In all her daydreaming, her legs were straddled open to permit her to step out of the limo. To most, discovering you were being watched would be like encountering a level of shame or disgrace. For Sharon, she just simply giggled to herself, deciphering "how much" he had gotten to see. It was definitely an early Christmas present..... A free one.

It was a simple example of something to be thankful for in the weeks to come. It was the third day of November today, the day before Mr. Tell Me Anything's birthday. In their family it was normally a holiday. He was real big on Birthdays. It was nothing for him to spend ten to twelve grand on any one of their kids on their special day. Sharon always thought it to be excessive but nothing she thought had seemed to matter due to the obvious fact that she made *none* of the money. It was his to blow. ....and blow it, he did. She sat back and watched at times as he blew it at warp's speed, all the while proclaiming that *you only live once!*

At any rate, the driver was a kind old man, with salt and pepper hair. She really couldn't describe his face to anyone because she only had eyes for *her* man. No one could understand it. They were perplexed by the idea that she could be around so many half-dressed athletes and not feel even a twitch when they brushed their calf muscles against her slickened legs or bear hugged her the way they did each other's wives. She felt nothing but sisterly and brotherly love. As a matter of fact, she thought enquirers to be silly and perverted with their thoughts. It was as if so many people had been failed by the idea of love and commitment. Sharon believed it still existed for those that believed in it. Love mattered to her. The universe seemed so fully established to her when she was around a special guy who made her forget about everyone and everything else. And Mr. Tell Me Anything was that guy for her. She lost all reasoning and sensibility when she looked into his brown eyes. Actually, his voice could command this loyalty from her being, too. He had her. She was not one for many distractions anyways. She wasn't perfect with her obvious flaws but she vowed to not invite distractions in because her struggle with her *own* man was enough.

"I don't need new dicks dangling in my head when I'm already confused."

She really thought sex was such a huge part of relationships. And the hugest part for her was some super head.

"If you ain't a head doctor then don't even waste your time. Oral pleasure....Yes....... I'm just saying......you gotta know how to do *something* to keep me satisfied. We might get old and the dick might collapse....then what the hell we gone do....get that head game tight!"

And her husband's game was tighter than ever. She hadn't met a guy younger or older who could chew it up as well as he could.

"Pure ecstasy!"

But whatever he wanted to do this night was fine with her.

"Make a list, baby."

And she was down for whatever.

"He can call me Sally or Sue or Mary Jane tonight because I'm not gonna hear him anyways. When I get my freak on, I'm gonna leave this place called Earth for a moment and forget my own name....his too for that matter. It's skin versus skin tonight. It's hard versus wet and nasty versus nastier, baby! Let's go!"

As Sharon began to talk to herself and think of the way he would feel when his hands touched her...she became so wet. The juices trickled down the crease of her perfect ass.

"That's exactly how he likes it......always wanting easy access to EVERYTHING! I am not a gay man or a porn star, but I find nothing wrong with a little anal action. Feels good to me...I'm a no limit soldier."

She drifted again to a place where there was nothing but more pleasure and excitement.

"Mam, are there any more stops?"

"Oh, no.....thank you."

She hit the privacy switch and the little black window closed slowly as all her windows opened. She needed some air. Nevertheless, he was going to be eyeing her down in the rearview mirror just because she indirectly let him peep into her cookie jar.

"I should be charging your old ass a fee of some sort... like a special preview deal or something. Ain't nothing in life free."

Since he was so interested, she wondered if Mr. Tell Me Anything would let him watch as she released her tension on his chiseled out face about three times. Yes, he was nasty like that. He usually paid girls to watch or he would ask one or two to join in. (secrets...oooh so many secrets). Sharon would do anything for her husband. But no girls tonight......just a dirty old man with roaming eyes.

"Maybe I'll ask him if he minds, surely he doesn't know a damned thing about YouTube..........too old for that. "

She thought that he would just be up there listening and wishing that some grandma would let him use his little blue pill tonight. Sharon truly believed in blue pills.

"People need help sometimes…...and it's nothing like a raging cookie jar looking for a cookie monster. I wonder do elderly people still get it on regularly. I hate to think of a cookie jar with cobwebs in it, laying right next to a former cookie monster. Age sucks! "

Sharon needed a forever lover that could roll over and puncture something forever and ever. "What would I do without dick? (Such a terrible thought) Not that I enjoy pain, but I do need to know that you *were there* to make it worthwhile. He travels way too much for an unwounded vagina. I need some recovery time in between road trips."

She had heard plenty of horrors of little dicks and the disgrace they cause themselves with horny females. Most women she knew didn't have time to be playing around with less than six inches. Her half-sister once told her that she wanted desperately to have something *tear her out the frame.* That idea stuck with Sharon because she felt sad knowing she had been deprived for so long. Her suggestion was that she used another hole that six inches could fill up, but she wasn't too big on taking up the a-hole.

"A girl has to do what a girl has to do…...but only with a man that I've got papers on. You're not going to just randomly ram your penis up my butt and I don't know where that thang is going after that. It may sound pretty nasty, but when you're married for a while, you gotta find ways to have some fun and sexual excursions with your body and your partner. My man loves his research, just trying to see *what* fits *where*. And if I let him…..he's game. You have to be careful though this day and time, anal sex is like a pre-punk test. If he wants to stick it up your ass *every* time, you got yourself a bit of a problem. And if you want it up your ass every time, you are gonna have a bigger problem called *diapers*. Nobody wants to walk around wearing diapers at my age. I definitely like the notion and the motion but I'll pass on the poor muscle control. I ain't that nasty. "She laughed at herself.

In all her booty thinking and evaluating, she decided she would let him stick it tonight. But only after he licked it right. If he was a good student he would remember the suck then lick then suck and lick some more concepts he scored high on last time he tested. Maybe he'll realize how much he misses her being away from him and have a better concept to apply. It's a special occasion. It's his birthday……so there you have it….an excuse to go *all out*.

"He'll be ramming it from the rear….settled….BIRTHDAY BOOTY! Let's go!"

She could see him now…..sucking around the hole until she had no other choice but to let him enter. The last episode was over in the Bahamas where he lost his mind sucking on her ass. The boy had no mercy. She couldn't

213

even feel her legs or her hands or her vagina and he hadn't even penetrated yet. He was sucking it and licking it like a hungry savage feasting on a cherry now-a-later. She couldn't escape, every time she crawled away; he apprehended her again and seized the hole ferociously with his vicious tongue. She was ambushed. Never had he done it so vigorously. She had told him that she watched the procedure on a flick and he had done it play by play as she related it. Before then, he often softly caressed it before entering to avoid her getting nervous and possibly backing out of the deal. It was almost as if he had to trick her into it with persuasive moves that directed her thoughts of anal penetration elsewhere. It's like he would kiss it and then ask if she loved him. Then he would gently whisper to her and require that she acknowledge that he could be trusted with the treasure of her fat ass. Then and only after this ritual, he would initiate ecstasy by inserting one finger for probing and another for sizing right before she started an automatic grinding motion to loosen things up a bit. Finally, when the coast was clear, he would slide of top of her and implant that peacemaker as far inside of her as her frame would allow. She was five feet ten inches tall...so you get the picture.

"Do your math....cause I'm taking it *all* tonight. *Birthday Booty* here we go! I'm gone top it off with these cufflinks."

She had had them custom made in Marina Del Rey at the Jeweler. They were always masters at their trade and so nice to them over the years. The owner really had a heart for people and some of the most exquisite taste she had ever seen. All she had to do was envision something and he immediately produced drawings and moldings…..and three weeks later….a perfect gift for her perfect man.

"He's gonna love these cufflinks."

She just obtained three more custom suits to add to his collections as well. But her haunch was that he would not have as much interest in the suits as the diamond and platinum cufflinks. They were an image of his first and last initials. Nobody had these on his team. She couldn't wait until he stunted on them all. She loved to see him in all his glory, making his way across the court after the game, dressed to impress in all her masterpieces. First, he addressed his fans. It was a routine. Then he scanned the arena until his gorgeous brown eyes meet hers with his perfect teeth gleaming from ear to ear. It had been that way since High School. He made that endless stride across the floor, seeking her embrace and the taste of her inner mouth. Often times, he plunged his tongue right down her throat, despite the spectators.

It was so exhilarating, just knowing that everyone could see their open acknowledgement of love for one another. Many often said that they were the perfect couple. Or at least, that's what they perceived. She would be the first to admit that there have been times where *what other's thought of them* was what she clung to to make it through the rough times. She couldn't let the kids down, or the fans.

"Besides, let them groupies vomit a little in their mouths every once in a while witnessing our love. That's right, he's mine.....keep dreaming while I'm wide awake and headed home with him and our warm bed waiting. You don't stand a chance."

As she began to discuss predators and their tactics, she lost her train of thought. "They are so pathetic and potentially dangerous at the same time. I have never seen so many women degrade themselves in the way they carry on on this level. It is like that they really believe that something will really be accomplished through sacrificing their souls and bodies to men who precisely *expect* them to with no regard as to what their feelings are. Surely, there's got to be a come to Jesus meeting somewhere for these type of creatures. You ain't fooling nobody or luring him in with your used goods. And if so...... It's temporary because men need more than sex on the road.....they need direction and strength outside the bedroom or in the limo in this case."

The limo was exquisite....... the newest edition out in the Cadillac world. He was always making sure that she had the best of everything even since the first day he bought her first promise ring in high school. It was unusually large for a cluster. Her family said it gave grandma's wedding ring a run for its money. How she had admired hers from her youth....and to think that her one year old mate had placed one of her very own on her finger as he devoted himself to her in his youth. She knew that she would be with him forever. Theirs was a love of the century, to be envied by most. She could remember asking him whether he had stolen it or not. He answered and reassured her that the Pawn Shop had great deals and perfect layaway plans. He had saved every penny he could for it. This man was priceless! "Who buys their high school love a ring that freaking large? " Though something about him scrapping to make her happy crossed her mind as *too much*, she thought his gift to be his way of proclaiming his manhood. He was staking his claim. She secretly made him take the money back though in small gifts back to him on weekends and her attempts to pay for their dates to the movies and out to their favorite wing joint. Always willing to give her last, he fell deeper in love with her. And she fell deeper for him even with his struggling financial situation. She had them. Never before had she met a man that she even wanted to spend her money on.....young or old. She prided herself in not being a biased or prejudiced person, but she did have to admit that men with larger budgets had been her previous forte. She found herself in a different arena now.....not caring about age or money.....just pure love and deep brown eyes.....She had met her match, the man who would change the rest of her life.

And tonight she would change his...

"I'm serving it up. Time to celebrate his special day and our love."

She knew he would love the cufflinks and the suits. She wanted so desperately for him to be happy. She had made him so miserable with the separation between them....always calling her to cry in the middle of the night about how cold it was in their bed without her naked body next to his. She felt so guilty. He hated the fact that they lived apart right now, spending hours and hours on the phone longing to see each other. But she promised that during Christmas break they were going to finish packing and move up North to Ohio to join him. Her thought was that they would know more about his upcoming contract by then. She would hate to drag the kids so far. It was more difficult the older they became, having to pick up and change their little lives so abruptly. They had become so much more involved in sports and their little friends now. It became harder and harder for them to say goodbye as the years came. Hopefully, he would do only one more contract and settle into retirement. She really could use his expertise with the boys on and off the court. The new teenager hormones had been something else to deal with.....especially knowing that all he had to do was *look* at them and they fell into submission. She on the other hand spent hours on end raising her voice to its limits in order to the get the laundry put away or the dishes placed into the dishwasher. A dad really made the difference in their home to her!

"Especially when he is as good as a man as mine. He must be rewarded tonight!"

Initially she was tormented with the delusion that the absence of his father and the stories she was told would affect his parenting skills and tolerance. But it was just the opposite; he was perfect when he was around.....which was not very often. He really needed to retire. She knew time was all he needed to excel. But who was she to make his decisions for him? She was just thankful that he didn't desert them as many of her friends had to raise their children alone and without much financial assistance from the fathers. It was hard to sit by and watch grown men not take care of their children. Sharon believed if a man didn't have any time.......he should at least have some money. Many times she wanted to complain about his poor time management but their age difference often softened her blows. She never wanted to make him feel that she was trying to run the show. He needed to be the man, her man. So, she let him, hardly ever challenging his authority. It all worked out in the wash.

When it came to his lavishing the kids with presents, she stepped aside as well. As he spent the moon, she put a small portion aside. She didn't believe his spending was too much to be concerned about. But she did battle with the fact that no one in his family had a J.O.B. but exactly *one* aunt and everyone else expected for him to pay their bills. She didn't understand how this could last......he was always the *go to* person. Sharon really didn't know if they all even understood the concept of retirement. But she guessed they would have a sit down in the months to come. She would speak up when the time came. And she would address the free loaders in due time. It was nothing more unattractive to her than a grown ass man living off of another grown ass man.

"The clan should prepare themselves for a cut-off. He'll probably say....."

"Missed you baby.........Happy Birthday!"

As she came to....He was standing over her...... all six feet and eleven inches of him in sweats and a smile. She could see his erection front and center. So she stretched her body inwards to meet his and pressed right up against it. He was as hard as a rock! Sharon knew that her night would be filled with passion and the kind of pain she had waited for all week.

Though she had been through so much with him, she knew that things were different now. They had even renewed their vows. The ceremony was unforgettable. Mr. Tell Me Anything had stood in front of a selected one hundred and twenty five guests to proclaim that he was "finally able to be the man that Sharon had deserved and that he vowed to never hurt her again or his kids." And she had believed her husband. She had loved the second marriage much better than the first because it had represented independence and maturity plus a more defined kind of love coming from her husband. It was a love that had made it through several hardships and an equal amount of women on the side. It was a marriage that had overcome the family and their misguided thoughts and it was a marriage that she believed was based on their new faith in God. It would last forever along with the feeling she had tonight after seeing him for the first time in eight days. Every time they made love was just like the very first time...just simply satisfying.

"I have some people for you to meet."

"Now.........Really?"

He didn't understand after all his years together with her that she hated the cold. Sharon had no intention of getting out of the cozy limousine until they had gotten home. They were parked outside of the practice arena and it was ten degrees plus icy. And.......there was nothing under the animal but her naked ass.

"Do I have a choice? Okay!"

"Come on, girl."

Everything he wanted was always okay, especially tonight. She hadn't realized how much she really missed him until she could smell his scent coming from underneath his sweats. She had longed to visit but the children had her bound to Tennessee with their full schedules. And now she was here, all alone and being dragged down a detour to meet people she didn't care to know tonight.

"This is our Head Coach."

He looked just as he did on television, but much clearer skin than she had remembered in his last broadcasted interview. He stood with his hand extended, announcing how pleased he was to meet her after all he had been told about her and the kids.

"You are all he ever talks about. And I can see why. Did any of the kids come up with you? Are you guys going to relocate soon?"

Sharon's patience wavered, "Damn coach, slow your roll, I'm here for the sex. I didn't engage in all this travel to have a 20/20 live interview with your ass about stuff I don't have answers to. I'm trying to jump up on something hard and long as soon as possible. It's been eight days. You got a girl feigning out here. Hurry up already with the questions. We can tour tomorrow." But she kept silent with a smile.

"So how's everyone adjusting to his being here?"

"Here we go again. We *ain't* adjusting. We in need of some dick! Why doesn't he get that? How does he think I mothered seven children? I need dick at all times. Shut your trap, coach. Cut through the bull." She remained sophisticated as usual.

"Oh, it's been a little tough, but we are so excited about being a part of your organization and can't wait to be here permanently. It's a great opportunity for us all. I simply love the city and its fan base."

Oh, this kind of stuff made his dick hard. He loved for her to work a room with her little cultivated self. Mixing and mingling and utilizing skills with a defined vocabulary pleased her man to the extreme.

"Yeah, baby......that's what I'm talking about,"Mr. Tell Me Anything whispered under his breathe.

Sharon was very skilled in joining his forces to enhance his image. And she was always happy to oblige, given the wretched truth concerning limited access to communication among adults. It's like her brain was trapped in *mommy land* until events such as these. She didn't want her inner honor student to waste away. So, what the hell.......

"So Coach, would it be too much to ask to take a tour of the facilities? I am especially fixated on wanting to see the locker room......since everyone is dressed."

Her flirtation made the coach's face turn flush red and her husband's dick grew another inch along with his smile.

"You can see anything you ask to see, young lady."

Men at this level treated women like trophies as if they had a stamp on them. A wife was the biggest trophy. If he was a jealous type...... like Mr. Tell Me Anything..... it was okay to talk about the trophy or gaze upon it as long as you didn't touch it. He only trusted people as far as he could see them, *including her.* So she always stayed in clear view to avoid confusion. In this case she waited for his command as she strolled from room to room asking the simplest questions she possibly could. As they traveled, the laughter rushed louder and louder into the building as the spectators grew in number. They had half the team following by now, all eager to see the trophy piece in person.

Her slickened legs were a must see. When they finally reached the lobby, she was invited to the player's lounge where food was being freshly prepared for them by a personal team chef on staff and eventually she was asked the question of the day. Obviously, the legs had inspired an overall inquiry as to what in the world everything else underneath the covering looked like. They were all panting like little thirsty puppies just waiting for the unveiling of his prize.

"Can I take your coat?"

"Oh no, thank you so much though."

"I'll put it right over there where it will be safe. Trust me I will keep an eye on it myself."

"Oh no, I'm a cold natured girl. I wouldn't want to catch flu and take it back to the kids. It's nowhere near this cold there."

"No, well I guess not. The last thing we would want is for you to do that."

"Baby are you *sure*? We all put all our jackets over there. You can sit by me, I'll keep you warm. You have to try the food, it's amazing. "He wanted them to see what he had invested in. The pressure was on. She never entered a place undone. He himself wanted to view his trophy tonight, as well.

And at this gesture, she positioned her body where only he could gaze upon it and exposed her concealed surprise."

"Damn! Coach Imma go ahead and get out of here. We are going to try to catch an early promised dinner for my birthday."

"Okay, you guys be good and have a good one."

She didn't know how he thought after eight excruciating days that it would be anything less than that. And off they went.....both racing to the chariot waiting.

"You came all the way here naked?"

"What's with all the questions? Don't worry about all that."

And she jammed his head in between her thighs. He began to pleasure her with his ritual of probing his mouthpiece backward and forward, up and down.....there

225

it was…..what she ventured there for……..orgasms. He was good for three to four minimum.

"You taste so damn good, girl. I love you."

"You just love these juices."

"Yeah, them, too."

"Why is it taking so long for us to get home?"

She swore the driver was torturing them. She needed to spread her legs farther apart so he could have better access to the center.

"I'm cheating myself here. How many lights to the house?"

"Is he going to stop at them all?"

"Baby did you really miss me?"

"Yeah, I can't believe you even asked me that. I can't even sleep without you here. I feel like my arm has been cut off. I'll be so glad when Christmas comes. The boys' beds come in tomorrow between ten and twelve noon."

"Good. They are so excited about the move."

Their life was going to be so great here. She had graduated to hating Georgia and somehow got stuck in Tennessee with the building of their dream home. She longed to be in his presence every waking moment. The renewal of their love was stronger than ever. She could feel the passion in his voice. He had missed her so much that even the coaching staff was aware of it. Her longed for changes had manifested in his new attitude and the gentleness of his words. She had him back now, the way it was supposed to be......without all the extras and the drama from every angle. They were good now. It was only a matter of time before the kids' transfer would be ready in school, nine weeks away. She nestled into thoughts of their grand future here in the North while his head nestled back down in between her legs once more to meet her with more desire.

"Can I help you with your bags?"

They were home. She hurled her mink across her shoulder blades and raced for the front door. Sharon was eager to smell the cinnamon scented candles and lunge into the plush living sofa covered in terracotta suede. It was their favorite place to make love. And there it was. In one motion, the refined animal was on the floor and she was butt naked with Mr. Tell Me Anything admiring her from end to end.

"Damn baby, you keeping it tight."

"I told you I was going to do it. She's two years old now. No more excuses. You like it?"

"Yeah, come here."

"Wait, pour us some wine and go get my bag, I have something for you."

"Where you going, girl?"

"To the bathroom, I have to use it."

"Come pee on me."

"Okay, boy you on some other stuff hunh. You can have whatever you like. Baby I aint going nowhere. I'm all yours for the next three days. Let me pee, please."

From inside the newly decorated powder room, she could hear him rummaging through the glasses to find two that matched. He knew she was particular about little things like that. Afterwards he took time to get the bag off the porch as she heard the front door close behind him and felt the crisp breeze whip underneath the poorly insulated door. He was back inside now.

"There goes the cork screw. Ooooooh I need him so such right now."

It was just as she had imagined it. You could cut the sexual tension between them with a knife....love was in the air. In less than two minutes she would surrender it all to her husband and love of her life. Sharon grew wet and impatient. The anticipation was too much to endure. (she gasps for air....then exhales)

"Boy, do I have a surprise for him."

She reached down inside her lambskin leather Chanel bag and pulled out a miniature container, supposing lip gloss, but actually, Vaseline. The airline had never expected it. Running a small portion across her posterior, she thought of how he would ram it up inside of her and go crazy at the thought of tormenting her fine ass body with his pain. She rubbed on a little more. This time she grew wetter. "Oh my God, we shouldn't ever wait this long again."

She washed her hands twice and began to rinse, she could hear him searching desperately for the right song.

"That's our favorite......Little does he know that I'm gone be screaming so damn loud that we ain't even gonna even hear that music."

Then she reaches over to throw away the paper towel and make her exit. And there it was, all wrapped in yellow.......the beginning of their end.

COMING SUMMER 2015

SHERRA
WRIGHT-ROBINSON
PRESENTS

Mr. Tell Me Anything

BOOK 2

Sherra Wright-Robinson is the ex-wife of former NBA basketball star Lorenzen Wright. She is also the CEO and founder of Born 2 Prosper Ministries along with Women Resurrected. This mother of six and new wife, has dedicated her life to helping others as a true humanitarian. Her vision is for all women to be set free from the chains of pain and disparity that holds them down. She believes in God and His miracles of love.

CPSIA information can be obtained
at www.ICGtesting.com
Printed in the USA
LVOW13s2212191217
560309LV00026B/530/P